"Please allow me to thank you properly for your kindness, Miss Price," Chase said. "We've rented a house here for the summer. Perhaps you could join us for dinner tomorrow night."

"We haven't decided how long we'll be staying in Scarborough. I'll send word if we're able to accept your kind offer."

He inclined his head in acceptance of Miss Price's dismissal, but his sister Phoebe's face crumpled. "Oh, but you can't leave! I just know we'll be the best of friends!"

Miss Price's smile was a gentle quirk of her peach-colored lips. "Then I'm certain our friendship will survive any absence. Good day, Lady Phoebe, my lord."

He took Miss Price's hand from his sister's and bowed over it. "Your devoted servant, Miss Price."

Chase could not shake the feeling that something wasn't aboveboard with the redoubtable Miss Price. She hurried up the beach as if the very forces of hell were at her heels. In his experience, a person who ran had a reason.

What was hers?

REGINA SCOTT

started writing novels in the third grade. Thankfully for literature as we know it, she didn't actually sell her first novel until she had learned a bit more about writing. Since her first book was published in 1998, her stories have traveled the globe, with translations in many languages including Dutch, German, Italian and Portuguese.

She and her husband of more than twenty years reside in southeast Washington State. Regina Scott is a decent fencer, owns a historical costume collection that takes up over a third of her large closet and she is an active member of the Church of the Nazarene. Her friends and church family know that if you want something organized, you call Regina. You can find her online blogging at www.nineteenteen.blogspot.com. Learn more about her at www.reginascott.com.

The Irresistible Earl

REGINA SCOTT

Love Inspired

Recycling programs
for this product may
not exist in your area.

LOVE INSPIRED BOOKS

ISBN-13: 978-0-373-82874-6

THE IRRESISTIBLE EARL

www.LoveInspiredBooks.com

Printed in U.S.A.

If anyone serves, he should do it
with the strength God provides, so that in all things
God may be praised through Jesus Christ.
—1 Peter 4:11b

To those I love, who never gave up on me:
Larry, Kristin, Meryl, Marissa,
Ammanda, Emily, Mom and Dad
and, most of all, my heavenly Father.
Thanks for giving me a chance to shine.

Chapter One

Yorkshire Coast, England, 1811

"Help! Help me!"

Meredee Price's head jerked up at the cry echoing across the waters of the North Sea. She'd been so intent on scanning the golden sands that she'd lost track of everything else. But if someone was in trouble, she had to help.

She scanned the area, eyes narrowed against the summer sun. The sweep of shore below the town of Scarborough was crowded with fashionable ladies in fluttering muslin gowns and gentlemen in high-crowned hats, strolling and chatting under a cloudless sky. The clear waves brushed against the bathing machines lined up in the surf to allow refined ladies to take the treatment of dipping into the cool waters. Each lady was attended by two burly women bathers, every machine pulled by two docile horses. All seemed calm, congenial.

"Someone, help!"

There! A girl floundered in the water near one of the bathing machines. The two lady bathers who would normally be attending her were struggling to lower a red-and-white canvas hood over the exit door of the white wood box on wide brown wheels. Their charge simply hadn't waited for their help. Already she'd plunged into water up to her chest. Whipping her honey-colored hair away from her pale face, she waved a thin hand at Meredee. "Help me!"

The cry pierced Meredee's heart, and she took a step forward.

Behind her she heard a sharp intake of breath. "Where are you going?" her stepmother demanded.

Meredee smothered a sigh. Quickly glancing over her shoulder, she saw that Evangeline Price was still shivering from her dip. Mrs. Murdock, one of their bathers, had her strong arms around her to steady Meredee's stepmother, and their other bather, Mrs. Lint, was standing ready to help, but Mrs. Price did not look comforted. Like Meredee, she stood in little more than a blue flannel shift, gray hair plastered to her thin cheeks, seawater streaming down her face and lapping at her waist.

"You haven't had your treatment yet," her stepmother protested. "And I will not pay our bathers to watch you look for shells!"

"It's not that," Meredee called. "Someone's in trouble."

"Oh, she'll be fine," Mrs. Murdock said in her booming voice, her vowels as long and fluid as the waters stretching out behind them. "Just put your foot down now, miss," she shouted to the girl. "It's not so deep here."

But the girl was clearly becoming panicked. Barely keeping her mouth above the water, she flailed her arms. "Hurry! Please!"

Meredee could see the fear on the girl's face, hear it in the sharp little cries. Surely someone should go to her aid! Mrs. Murdock evidently thought better of her words, for she started forward. But Mrs. Price held her back, clinging to her and Mrs. Lint as if afraid the sea would rise and swallow her too. And there was no help anywhere else. Up and down the beach, the dandies and fine ladies who flocked to Scarborough for the summer were staring, pointing.

"Will no one help?"

At the sound of the anguished cry, one of the horses reared in its traces. Meredee gasped as the wagon jerked and swung to one side, knocking one of the bathers into the waves with a splash. The other clung to her perch, face white, as the wagon teetered on two wheels, overshadowing the girl, who stared up at it as if in a trance.

Enough! Meredee didn't wait another second. She waded over, seized the girl under the arms, and dragged her away from the wagon. Still the girl struggled, her slender body colliding with Meredee's. Her fear was very nearly contagious. The sand shifted under Meredee's feet; the waves broke against her back. The cold was nothing compared to the chill inside her.

Help me, Lord. I can't lose someone else at Scarborough.

She widened her stance and tightened her grip. "You're safe," she said against the girl's temple. "I have you." She nearly cried out in relief when the girl went limp in her arms. "Just put down your feet."

Wet skirts brushed hers as the girl complied.

"There," Meredee said soothingly, as much to calm the girl as to settle her own pulse. "You see? We're fine."

She released her hold, and the girl turned to face her. Her eyes were deep brown and wide with shock. "Oh, thank you! You saved my life!"

Meredee shook her head, but, before she could protest, one of the girl's bathers waded up. "Everything all right here?"

"This woman is a savior," the girl declared. "I might have drowned if it wasn't for her."

The bather's face tightened. Meredee knew that even a rumor that the bather had been negligent might keep others from patronizing her. Rumors flew fast in the little resort town and quickly grew out of proportion.

"You know, you might have drowned at that," Meredee's bather declared as she splashed up to them, Meredee's stepmother in tow. "A body can drown in just a few feet of water. That's why you have us."

"And that's why we pay perfectly good money for the treatment," Mrs. Price said with a pointed look at Meredee. The refrain was all too familiar. Though her scholar father had left the family with a comfortable living, his second wife refused to allow a single penny to leave her fingers until she had wrung the life from it.

As if the other bather sensed that Meredee was about to be scolded, she stepped closer. "Ah, but look at your daughter, now. Perhaps we should hire her out. Regular mermaid, isn't she?"

Meredee was certain her cheeks would have reddened in a blush if they hadn't been tingling with the cold. Her thick, wavy hair might qualify as golden and her late father had always said her eyes were the color of the sea in a storm, but she was hardly a mermaid. Her interests in Scarborough lay cradled in the sands, not out among the waves.

"She is not my daughter," Mrs. Price said, eyes narrowing. "I'm quite certain I am entirely too young to have a daughter of five and twenty."

That she had a son two years older by a previous marriage did not seem to trouble her. It was only Meredee she found such a terrible burden.

Lord, give me patience.

"Now, come along," Mrs. Price said, her lips a determined shade of blue. "You can see this person is fine."

The girl didn't look fine. She clutched her soaked gown to her chest, trembling. Meredee's heart went out to her, but she knew her duty lay with her stepmother. She offered the girl a smile before turning to go, but the girl reached out for Meredee's arm. "No, wait. I must know the name of my savior."

The title felt entirely wrong. "I know only one Savior," Meredee told her, "but my name is Meredee Price."

"Lady Phoebe Dearborn," she replied, voice trembling, as well. "And I shall be forever in your debt."

Meredee thought her stepmother might try to curry favor now that she knew the girl was titled, but Mrs. Price's financial concerns proved paramount. "Then perhaps you would be so good as to pay our bathers," she put in, nose in the air. "They charge by the hour, you know, and we are taking up a good deal of their time."

Lady Phoebe dropped her gaze and her hold on Meredee's arm. "Of course. I'm sure my brother would be delighted. I'm terribly sorry to have inconvenienced you."

Meredee couldn't bear to see the girl so forlorn. She enveloped her in a hug, the chill of the bathing costumes warming for a moment, then stepped back.

"It was no trouble, I assure you. Perhaps we'll see each other in town."

An answering smile lit Lady Phoebe's dark eyes.

"I suppose we've forfeited Meredee's time for a cure," Mrs. Price said, heaving a martyred sigh as Meredee followed her and Mrs. Murdock back to their bathing machine.

"Not at all," Mrs. Murdock said with a wink to Meredee. "I'll be more than happy to give Miss Price the cure, no charge. Anything for the savior of Scarborough Bay."

Meredee smiled at her but shook her head. "No, I wouldn't want Mrs. Price to take a chill." She gazed down into the waters one last time, but the movements of the horses and bathers had so muddied her view that she knew she'd never spot what she'd been searching for now. Suppressing a sigh, she climbed the few steps into the bathing machine for their trip to the shore.

Mrs. Price's mood improved along the way as Meredee helped her into her underthings and the sprigged muslin gown that had been hanging from pegs on the white enameled walls of the cozy wooden box. But then, Meredee had found, her stepmother's moods generally improved as long as Meredee devoted herself to the older woman's comfort.

"I suppose Scarborough isn't the end of the world," Mrs. Price said with a final shiver. She took a seat on the bench that lined one wall as Meredee began changing, as well. "Still, I never intended to see this place again. I cannot imagine what Algernon was thinking to bring us here. Surely there are more fashionable bathing places."

Oh, there were no doubt more fashionable bathing places—like the prince's favorite summer haunt, Brighton. Still, each summer since the 1600s, Scarborough had attracted people from the aristocracy to the merchant class to tarry along its cool shores, drink of the famous healing spa waters, bathe in the sea and congregate at the spa house, Assembly Rooms, or St. Mary's Church. Even now Meredee had heard the governor of the spa, William Barriston, chortling that the population of the town had doubled to nearly seven thousand souls.

No, her stepbrother didn't need any more crowds than the ones at Scarborough. Meredee had been the one who had convinced him to make for the Yorkshire Coast when he'd come to her in a panic a fortnight ago. She still could not understand what he'd done to so anger someone as powerful and vindictive as the Earl of Allyndale. People generally liked Algernon's beaming smile and charming conversation, even if they shook their heads over his colorful choice of clothing. She could not imagine why Lord Allyndale would threaten a duel, but she certainly wasn't willing to stand by and see her stepbrother killed.

And she had a promise to keep in Scarborough, one she'd neglected to fulfill for five years. What she really needed was a good low tide, preferably after a decent storm. And an hour or so to herself.

But she wasn't likely to be left alone anytime soon. As Mrs. Murdock opened the door to help Meredee and Mrs. Price from the shadows of the bathing machine onto the dry sands, a cheer went up. Meredee blinked into nearly two dozen faces. It seemed as if every notable touring the crescent of the beach had heard Lady Phoebe's cries and watched Meredee's rescue. Now they gathered from the spa house at the southern tip to the lighthouse sheltering under the watchful eye of Scarborough Castle, just to congratulate her.

She wanted to shrink back into the box. She was supposed to help Algernon remain in hiding, keep from calling undue attention to themselves. What had she done?

Mrs. Price did not seem worried. She preened at the attention, patting her damp gray tresses and putting on a long-suffering smile. "Yes, yes, dreadful, isn't it?" she lamented to the plump countess in breezy white muslin who was the first to step forward. "I'm certain the poor girl would have drowned if I hadn't directed Meredee to rescue her."

Meredee could only wish for rescue herself. Sun hot on her cheeks, she had to give an accounting of her stunning heroism to a country squire from Devonshire, an Italian nobleman, two knights of the bath with wives in tow and a silk merchant from Carlisle before another man elbowed his way to the front. He was tall and powerfully built, with hair nearly the color of the sands and eyes like the North Sea. The others stepped aside when they saw that he was interested in questioning her. From the scowl on his craggy face, she would have been tempted to flee as well, if Lady Phoebe hadn't been at his side.

Though the girl could not have reached the shore much sooner, she had traded her flannel bathing costume for a high-waisted muslin gown embroidered all over with yellow daisies. Her damp hair curled into waves around her lovely face. Meredee, in her simple blue cotton gown, hair in a braid down her back, felt like a country cousin beside her.

"I simply had to thank you again, Miss Price," the girl declared in awed tones. "And so did my brother. Mrs. Price, Miss Meredee Price, may I present my brother, Chase Dearborn, Lord Allyndale."

Chase watched as both women blanched. Mrs. Price went so far as to take a step back, but Miss Price's hand on her arm kept her from fleeing. Though he knew a few men who would run at the sight of him, he couldn't recall a time when a lady felt the need to escape.

And they were certainly ladies. In fact, Mrs. Price reminded him of his late mother—high jutting cheekbones; long aristocratic nose; narrow, elegant frame. But he had never met anyone quite like Meredee

Price. She had the thick golden hair and wise gray eyes of a Saxon princess, yet the impressive curves of a heroine in one of Botticelli's paintings. He could easily imagine her lifting the fragile Phoebe from the waves, or riding into battle against the Norse forces.

She dropped her gaze, dipped a quick curtsy and spoke in soft tones, with a musical lilt. "An honor to meet you, my lord. But I wish you would not dwell on what happened in the waves. It was truly nothing."

The rest of the crowd insisted on her heroism, which only set her cheeks to blushing. Was she truly a shy, retiring creature, then? And why did that so disappoint him? After meeting any number of young society misses while escorting his sister, he'd resigned himself to being surrounded by shy, retiring creatures.

"Nothing!" Phoebe cried, reaching out to snatch up Meredee's hand and press it close. "How can you say that! I could not live with myself unless I found a way to thank you properly. You saved my life!"

Normally Chase would have stepped in to temper his sister's unbounded enthusiasm, but in this case he rather thought she had the right to it. Despite his efforts to raise his sister, who was twelve years his junior, the girl seemed to invite disaster. He hadn't been able to see her from where he had waited along the shore, but he'd heard Phoebe's cries for help and could well believe it had taken Miss Price's intervention to save his sister.

"Please allow me to thank you property for your kindness, Miss Price," he said as the poor lady visibly squirmed in Phoebe's fervent grip. "We've rented a house here in Scarborough for the summer. Perhaps you could join us for dinner tomorrow night, along with your mother, of course."

"I am not her mother," Mrs. Price put in, laying a hand on the woman's arm and acting as if she would tug her away from Phoebe. "And I think we truly must go."

Meredee Price did not seem agitated to find herself the rope in the middle of a tug-of-war contest. "What my stepmother means," she said calmly, gaze rising to meet his and serving to fix him in his place, "is that we haven't decided how long we'll be staying in Scarborough. We may depart this very afternoon. I'll send word if we're able to accept your kind invitation."

He'd been mistaken. No Saxon princess this, but clearly the queen and just as regal. He inclined his head in acceptance of her dismissal, but Phoebe's face crumpled. "Oh, but you can't leave! I just know we'll be the best of friends!"

Miss Price's smile was a gentle quirk of her peach-colored lips. "Then I'm certain our friendship will survive any absence. Good day, Lady Phoebe, my lord."

Chase could see the protest building in the stubborn set to Phoebe's little chin. He refused to allow her to stage a greater scene than she had already done. He took Miss Price's hand from his sister's and bowed over it. "Your devoted servant, Miss Price."

She curtsied more fully this time, and when she rose he was surprised to see a shadow cross her eyes, like a raven swooping across storm clouds. Although Phoebe and Mrs. Price made their farewells in polite tones, Chase didn't think it was his imagination that Meredee Price's grip on her stepmother's arm was every bit as fevered as Phoebe's as they hurried up the beach for the shops and houses beyond.

He only wondered who she was running away from—Phoebe or him.

Chapter Two

"What were you thinking?" Mrs. Price lamented as they hurried along the crowded streets that led through the town. "We cannot dine with Lord Allyndale! We daren't stay in Scarborough another minute! Oh, my poor Algernon—hunted from pillar to post!"

"Calm yourself," Meredee said with assurance she was far from feeling. "Lord Allyndale obviously saw no connection between us and the Algernon Whitaker who so offended him."

"Well, of course not," Mrs. Price huffed. "Nor would he have noticed us if you hadn't made a spectacle of yourself!"

Meredee bit back a retort. Angry words would do none of them any good now. She had only been trying to help. And even if she had known the girl was the sister of Algernon's sworn enemy, she wouldn't have let Lady Phoebe struggle. She'd never been able to overlook the pain or fear of others; it was in her very nature to offer help when it was needed.

"Be that as it may," she said, leading her step-mother past the shops overflowing with bright fabrics, exotic scents and fine literature, "we have been discovered. We have only to explain the situation to Algernon, and I'm certain he'll see the wisdom of escaping."

Mrs. Price nodded and said no more, as if she needed her breath to climb the remaining way up the hill to the Bell Inn, where they had taken rooms. Meredee was just as glad for her silence. She could not stop thinking about their meeting with Lord Allyndale.

When Algernon had confided to her a fortnight ago in their London town house that he feared Allyndale would challenge him to a duel, the man he'd described had been a monster. "He's completely unreasonable," he'd fretted, pacing about the yellow silk–draped bedchamber that had been hers since she had finished her schooling. "There's no use talking to him or begging his pardon. If he issues a challenge, I'm a dead man."

"But the magistrates," she'd protested from her four-poster bed where he'd found her that night. "Surely you could go to them, explain the situation. Dueling is against the law."

Algernon smiled at her as if he envied her her innocence. "Dueling may be against the law, but the magistrates will turn deaf as soon as they hear who's involved. Allyndale is too powerful. Word at White's is that he's already forced one fellow to flee for the Continent."

"But why?" Meredee asked, fisting her bedclothes, never doubting the word of those who thronged London's most famous gentlemen's club. "Why would he seek your ruin?"

"It doesn't matter," her stepbrother had replied, pausing in his pacing to meet her gaze. His deep blue eyes had been mirrors of despair. "He has taken me in dislike, and he will not rest until he's made my life hell."

Meredee shivered, remembering. Lord Allyndale was obviously a man who toyed with the lives of others just for the thrill of power. She could not allow Algernon to fall into his clutches. She'd proposed the plan to flee and the place to hide, sure that the earl would soon find someone else to torment. Yet here he was, on their very doorstep!

She had to admit she was a bit disappointed.

She'd expected eyes that flashed with dark intentions, a face slack with dissipation, a body gross with indulgence. But Lord Allyndale was well-formed, with broad shoulders that filled his tailored coat and long legs that showed well in chamois breeches. Her father had always said that evil could hide behind a winsome smile, but she still thought some trace should be visible, if only to warn away those with the insight to look for it.

She had looked today, but she could not see the creature Algernon feared. Lord Allyndale's smile held a pride and love for his sister; the way his arm draped around her shoulders spoke of a desire to protect her. And the way he'd gazed into Meredee's eyes—so sure, so deep—why it had nearly taken her breath away.

Had she mistaken the name Algernon had uttered with such despair? Or could her stepbrother have misunderstood the earl's intentions?

When they reached the inn and sought out her stepbrother, she wasn't surprised to find him still in the little whitewashed bedchamber under the eaves. While Meredee and Mrs. Price had been willing to rise early to shop and then to bathe in the sea, Algernon was only now peering into the mirror over his mahogany washstand in his shirtsleeves and scraping his lathered chin with a razor.

"Allyndale, here?" He dropped the razor into the porcelain washbowl, heedless of the soapy water that splashed his otherwise spotless yellow pantaloons. As Meredee carefully closed the door behind her, he turned to stare at her and his mother. "Are you certain? Did he speak of me?"

"He did not," Mrs. Price put in. "And thank God for that!"

Meredee could only agree. Of course, she would not have been so bold as to ask God for Algernon's safety. God never answered her prayers for large things—her mother's recovery from the carriage accident that had taken her life when Meredee was only eight, her father's healing from the illness that racked his body and cut short his studies as a conchologist, even her own situation with Mrs. Price. Now she just asked for little things, like patience.

"Lord Allyndale did not connect us with you," Meredee told her stepbrother and explained how they had met the earl.

When she finished, she fully expected Algernon to wipe the foam from his face and set about packing. Instead, he began pacing the little inn room, taking three strides from the multipaned window to Meredee's side where she perched on a ladder-backed chair next to his narrow bed. It seemed her stepbrother's mind only worked properly when propelled by the energy of his long legs.

"But Lady Phoebe was all right?" he asked.

Trust Algernon to worry about the pretty girl first. "I sincerely doubt she was in any danger," Meredee assured him. "I am no hero."

He sent her a grin that broadened his narrow face and lit his deep blue eyes like sapphires in candlelight. "Well, you've been known to bail me out a time or two."

"And I haven't?" Mrs. Price immediately protested.

Algernon's smile softened. "Certainly you have,

Mother. I wonder sometimes how I manage to tie my cravat without advice from the two of you."

"Then listen to me now," Mrs. Price ordered. "We should leave. It's the only way to be certain we're safe."

Meredee bit back a sigh. Her stepmother was right. But when would she get to the Yorkshire Coast again? She'd been suggesting the trip for five years, but Mrs. Price saw no need to return to the area where her second husband had met his end. Yet Meredee could only keep her promise to her father by coming here.

"Not necessarily," Algernon said, holding up a hand. "Regardless of how Meredee feels about the matter, Lady Phoebe clearly believes Meredee saved her life. We may be able to use that to our advantage."

Meredee felt as if the room had chilled and rubbed one hand along the sleeve of her blue cotton gown. "What do you mean?"

"Yes, Algernon," Mrs. Price demanded. "You insist we flee this fellow, at considerable inconvenience I might add, and now you wish to embrace him?"

"Not me, Mother," Algernon replied patiently. "Meredee."

"Me!" Meredee hated the squeak in her voice. Why couldn't she have a solid voice, a commanding voice? Her voice was high and soft, like a bird chirping, and as easily ignored, just as her family ignored her now.

"Meredee?" Mrs. Price shook her head, gray curls bouncing. "Unthinkable. I will not allow you to put her in danger. Besides, I do not know how I should get on without her."

As Mrs. Price was neither infirm nor forgetful, Meredee could not see herself as so indispensable. Of course, it would cost her stepmother more money if she actually had to hire a companion instead of relying on Meredee for every little thing.

"We must all make sacrifices, Mother," Algernon said as if agreeing with Meredee's thoughts.

"But exactly what sacrifices must I make?" Meredee asked.

His smile was kind. "Nothing onerous, I promise. Merely accept his offer. Dine with him and Lady Phoebe. See if you can get him to confess why he's come to Scarborough."

Algernon had no idea what he was asking. Dine with his enemy? Surely her face, her least word would betray her. She was certain that Lord Allyndale had taken her measure on the shore, but the way he had touched her hand, bowed over it as if she were a great lady, had confused her more than anything else. The look in his eyes said he esteemed her.

All because she'd had the good sense to tell his sister to set down her feet.

Meredee shook her head. "No, I can't do it. Even if Lord Allyndale is a monster, I cannot lie to him.

If he asks me about you, I'll be the one making a confession."

"Ungrateful girl!" Mrs. Price cried, shaking a finger at her. "And where would you live if Algernon wasn't so generous?"

Meredee stared at her hands, clenched together in her lap. She couldn't bear to see the censure in her stepmother's gaze. She didn't understand why her father hadn't made provision for her in his will, outside of leaving her his collection of seashells. Algernon had inherited the entire estate. Both Mrs. Price and she lived on his largesse. And she was truly grateful for Algernon's kindness.

"Mother, please," Algernon said. "Meredee is the best sister a fellow could ask. I probably wouldn't be alive without her wise counsel." He walked to the chair and knelt in front of her, forcing Meredee to meet his gaze.

"Have I asked too much of you?" he said softly. "Is it such a terrible duty to go to a fine house, eat fine food, be treated like the lady you were meant to be?"

Meredee felt tears burning her eyes, and she dashed them away with one hand. "You make it sound like a party, but all I see is a battle."

"And who better suited to go into battle on the side of righteousness than my brave sister?" he insisted. "Who nursed Father through two years of pain and suffering? Who helped Mother see him buried? Who even now keeps us all from going mad in times of trouble?"

"Kind words," Meredee countered with a sniff. "But they would be much more convincing if they hadn't been uttered from behind a face covered in foam."

Algernon barked a laugh and rose. "See? I knew you'd come around." He strode to the washstand, picked up the linen towel hanging there and wiped off his face. "So, you'll do it?" he asked, his gaze meeting hers in the mirror. "You'll have dinner with Lord Allyndale and see what you can learn?"

Meredee sighed. "Yes, I'll do it. I'll go pen a note to the earl right now. May God have mercy on us all."

Chase could not shake the feeling that something wasn't aboveboard with the redoubtable Miss Price. She'd run from him at the beach as if the very forces of hell were at her heels. In his experience, a person who ran had a reason.

What was hers?

A few pointed questions of the crowd before he took Phoebe home were enough to learn Miss Price's direction. He thought about her actions all the way home and wasn't surprised when a boy brought a politely penned note from her accepting his invitation to dine. Even in writing Miss Price evinced none of the sentiment his mother and sister preferred. An intriguing woman. Surely a call at the Bell Inn would not be too much attention for the woman who had saved his sister's life.

He had just started out from the house he had rented for the summer when he spotted Sir Trevor Fitzwilliam coming up the drive. He hadn't stopped to think when he'd invited his friend to join him and Phoebe in Scarborough. He and Trev had both had reasons for wanting to avoid London for a time. Now it struck him as singularly good luck that he had someone as savvy as Trevor in train.

"Out for a ride?" Trev asked, back straight as a soldier's in his navy coat. He patted his horse, Icarus, on the neck.

"I'm on an errand," Chase replied. "But you're welcome to join me. In fact, I'd appreciate your insights."

Trevor's green eyes lit, and he pulled the black gelding in alongside Chase's bay mare. "What's the to do? A new tract of land? A faster horse? A better coat?"

"My estate is larger than needed, my horse is fast enough and there's nothing wrong with my coat," Chase countered.

Trevor adjusted his top hat on his dark head and avoided looking at Chase's bottle-green coat. "As you say."

"Much more of that, and you can whistle for your supper."

"Don't I usually?" Trev replied, with an edge of bitterness Chase could not like. Trevor's desires frequently outstripped his pockets. Chase was more than happy to house and feed the friend he'd known since his school days, but he suspected that Trevor chafed at the kindness. That was one of the reasons the baronet had begun taking on inquiries for society, to avoid living on his friends' largesse.

As they rode through the cobbled streets among elegant town houses and square stone inns, Chase filled him in on the afternoon's adventure.

"And I take it the lady piqued your interest," Trevor said as they rounded the corner and sighted the Bell Inn just ahead.

Chase shrugged. "There's more to the woman than strength and vitality."

Trev's dark brows shot up. "Strength? Vitality? Do you speak of a woman or a horse you're considering purchasing?"

"A lady to be sure," Chase answered with a smile. "But something about her doesn't set right."

"Of what do you suspect her?"

Chase scowled at him. "Am I that much of a tyrant that I must suspect everyone I see of dark motives?"

Trevor merely eyed him.

Chase sighed. "Very well, I admit that I wondered why she of all the people acted. At least a dozen women were bathing this afternoon along the shore, with a similar number of women assisting them. Why did she alone rush to Phoebe's aid?"

"Perhaps she sought to bring herself to your notice, ingratiate herself to the Dearborn family."

"And what a coxcomb I am to suspect it, I know."

"You have cause," Trevor said quietly.

Chase shifted his weight on the saddle. He didn't need the reminder of how one man had nearly destroyed his sister. He would not let anyone hurt Phoebe. *You honored me with intelligence, strength, and resources, Lord. Give me the wisdom to use them.*

They rode into the coaching yard of the Bell Inn, a respectable two-story stone building with flower boxes under the multipaned windows. The common room inside was neat and clean. The polished oak tables and ladder-backed chairs welcomed visitors to chat before the rough-stone hearth taking up much of the left wall. A word to the landlord was enough to see their horses stabled and tankards placed before them in a quiet private parlor while they waited for a boy to take word up to Miss Price and her stepmother. Miss Price returned alone, in a remarkably short time, hurrying through the door as if keeping Chase waiting was the worst sin imaginable.

She still wore the blue dress, though she'd had time to wind her hair up into a braided coronet that suited her. She dipped a quick curtsey. "Lord Allyndale. We didn't expect to see you until tomorrow."

Chase bowed over her hand and found it trembling. Was he such a fearsome thing then? He glanced at Trevor, but his friend was frowning. He took a step back and bumped Trev's leg on purpose. "May I present my good friend, Sir Trevor Fitzwilliam, baronet?"

She curtsied again, and Trev wiped the frown from his face and bowed. "Forgive the interruption, Miss Price," he said as he straightened, "but I had to thank you personally for saving Lady Phoebe's life. The Dearborns have been good friends for years, and I take your assistance as a personal favor."

Putting it on a little thick, Chase thought. But Miss Price merely lowered her gaze to the shine of Trev's black high-topped boots.

"You are too kind," she murmured. "I'm sure Lady Phoebe must have realized by now how little I did to help her."

"On the contrary," Chase assured her, "she is effusive in her praise. You have made a conquest, Miss Price."

She looked up then, meeting his gaze, and once more he felt put firmly in his place. "I didn't intend to conquer anyone, my lord. It was very kind of you to visit, but I fear I cannot stay. This afternoon's events overtired my stepmother. I must return to her side immediately. Good day."

She dipped one last graceful curtsey and slipped

from the room while Chase and Trev were still in midbow.

Trev met Chase's puzzled gaze. "For a woman out to trap you, she doesn't have a great deal of use for your company," his friend pointed out. "In fact, I've never seen a woman more intent on resisting your least charm."

Chase shook his head and motioned Trev out of the room ahead of him. "Then perhaps I will have to become irresistible, for I intend to learn everything I can about the formidable Miss Price."

Chapter Three

Meredee didn't know whether to be pleased or perplexed. What did it mean that Lord Allyndale had brought his close friend to meet her only hours after being introduced? She could not credit that she'd made such an impression on the earl. They'd only spoken a few sentences!

And then there was Sir Trevor Fitzwilliam, easily one of the handsomest men in Scarborough, with his raven hair and square jaw. She was no student of fashion, but even she could tell that his navy coat had been cut by a London tailor. Still, she could not be sure of his character. His lips might smile, but calculation crouched in his cool, green eyes.

She'd have been tempted to stay safely in her little room, but Algernon was certain that she and Mrs. Price should not alter their habits to avoid any possibility of suspicion. So, while her stepbrother cooled his heels at the inn, she accompanied Mrs. Price to the spa house the next morning.

The town of Scarborough ran along a hillside and sloped gently down in the center toward the shore like the neckline of a frock. The headland that held Scarborough's castle (and several regiments) separated the more rustic North Bay from the South and sheltered the harbor and fishing fleet.

Scarborough's spa house sat to the south. The long, low building lay close to the shore and could be reached by driving along the sands. Mrs. Price insisted on puffing down the tree-shadowed path that wound down the cliff. Meredee enjoyed the views of the sea on the way down, but some days she'd have far preferred to lounge in a sedan chair like many of the fashionable ladies and let someone else's legs carry her back up.

The spa house was its usual hub of activity that morning as they entered the receiving room. Already ladies in bright flowered bonnets sat on the harp-backed chairs that lined the pale green walls and chatted. Their voices rose and fell like the sound of the waves on the shore just outside. Couples promenaded around the polished wood floor or paused to gaze out the row of clear glass windows at the sea. Many people were already making for a door at the far end of the room, which led to a flight of dark stone stairs and a terrace that held the two wells of healing spring water for which the town was famous.

"And here is the savior of Scarborough Bay," proclaimed William Barriston as they entered the receiving room. The governor of the spa was a tall, thin man with an engaging grin who was rumored to have attained the stunning age of eighty-eight years by drinking daily of the waters. Meredee had known him since she was a baby. His bright blue eyes twinkled in his wrinkled face as he approached her now.

"What is this I've been hearing about you from Mrs. Barriston?" he said, shaking his long finger at her. "Quite the heroine, eh?"

Meredee wasn't surprised that his wife had told him the tale. The governor's third wife was the area's most accomplished gossip, and someone Meredee avoided whenever possible.

"I have received no less than five requests for introductions already," he continued. "One fellow even offered me a gold piece." He rubbed his gloved hands together gleefully.

"It was nothing," Meredee insisted. "I wish everyone would stop dwelling on it."

He patted the shoulder of her jonquil-colored short jacket. "You are the latest seven days' wonder, my dear. I advise you to make the most of it."

Impossible. She had to avoid undue attention, for Algernon's sake if not her own sanity. She'd never liked being the center of attention. She didn't come to the spa to preen.

Not so Mrs. Price. She immediately set about

greeting everyone they knew, from portly Mr. Cranell, who was an old friend of Meredee's father's, to the bold countess who had introduced herself yesterday after Meredee had rescued Lady Phoebe. Meredee smiled politely through every conversation, trying to keep from fidgeting. She'd have much rather cheered Mr. Openshaw, who had lost an arm serving on the Peninsula, or the country squire crippled with gout. The sadness in their eyes, their tenacity in adversity, spoke to her heart. She felt more at home with them than with the fashionable ladies who wrinkled their noses at the strong metallic taste of the waters they sipped, all the while their gazes roamed the room like those of lionesses intent on their prey.

Ah, but she shouldn't judge them. She had been told time and again—by her father, by her governess—that the surest way to a secure future was to find a wealthy husband. Even Mrs. Price understood that. She'd already buried two husbands, and still she batted her thinning lashes, swished her pale muslin skirts and giggled like a girl at something the widowed Mr. Cranell said, making the old fellow turn as red as the tops of his boots. As soon as she could, Meredee excused herself and went to stand by the windows, gazing out at the sea.

She could hear the waves through the glass as they tumbled over the sands. Already men in dark coats and women with pale parasols wandered the shore. But Scarborough's bays never failed to remind her of her father. How many times had he trod those golden sands, head bowed, hands clasped behind his black coat, while she scurried along behind him, hoping she might find a way to be useful to him.

"Wait for me, Papa!" she'd cry.

But as usual, he hadn't waited. He'd gone on ahead of her and left her behind, no more sure of her purpose.

"Such dark thoughts on this fine day," Lord Allyndale said quietly beside her.

Meredee took a deep breath and composed her face. He had no need to know anything more about her. In fact, the more she said, the more likely he was to connect her with Algernon. She turned and smiled at him. "Good morning, my lord. And how is your dear sister?"

"Fine, as you can see," he said, nodding to where Lady Phoebe was squealing with delight over another young lady's velvet jacket. His sister wore a pink muslin gown with ruffles at the hem that fluttered as she moved. Her straw bonnet was covered with a profusion of ribbons and silk flowers, making it look as if she had brought spring with her. The earl himself looked more somber, dressed in a navy coat and buff-colored breeches above gleaming boots.

"You don't seem to have thrown off yesterday's events as easily," he said. "If I may, Miss Price, you look tired."

Was that concern in his voice? Why should he

care? "And do you flatter all the young ladies this way, my lord?" Meredee countered.

He chuckled, a warm rumble that was hard to resist. "I'm afraid I'm not good at doing the pretty. Some other fellow would quote you poetry or the Bard. 'She walks in beauty like the night,' or some such."

"I've never been all that much for poetry," Meredee admitted. *No, it's more likely quiet concern that will be my undoing.*

"That we have in common, then. What do you prefer to read?"

Meredee eyed him. His head was cocked, and the light through the windows touched his sandy hair with gold and highlighted the planes on his face. Nothing in his look or his attention said he was teasing her. How extraordinary! But she doubted he'd look so attentive if he knew the truth. Most men would be aghast at her reading material. Even her stepmother turned up her nose. Only one other man had ever listened to her prose on, and she'd done her best to forget him. She would be safer admitting to the occasional gothic novel, which she did enjoy.

"Ah," he said just as she realized she had probably been silent too long. "Perhaps you prefer not to read."

She refused to leave him with that impression. "Most likely I read too much, my lord. I love history, and the latest scientific discoveries. I recently found a copy of Mr. Humboldt's treatise on his travels to the equatorial regions of the South American continent. It was most inspiring."

She waited for his eyes to glaze over, to hear him murmur polite excuses and hurry away as generally happened when she shared her pastimes. But he merely leaned closer, his eyes lighting. "And do you adhere to his theory that the earth's magnetic field varies between the poles and the equator?"

"He was most persuasive, though I should like to see his observations duplicated on the African continent. Flora and fauna would be more of a challenge there, I think."

He straightened and beamed at her, suddenly looking as young and carefree as Algernon. "My thoughts exactly. And what of more practical matters? Are you a staunch supporter of Hannah More or do your tastes run to Mary Wollstonecraft?"

"Must it be one or the other? Mrs. More instructs us to read the Bible and think on how we can best serve the Lord. Mrs. Wollstonecraft insists that only a woman who uses her intelligence can truly find her purpose. I do not see that the two contradict each other."

He laughed. "I'd like to see you explain that to them."

She couldn't help but smile. "I suppose they would find a great deal to argue about. What of you, my lord? Which do you find more useful?"

His gaze traveled to where his sister was even now blushing as a tall, angular young man bowed over her hand. "The Bible guides us in our lives, but every woman should use her intellect to ensure her future. Excuse me, Miss Price."

She curtsied, but he was already striding across the room to his sister's side. As Meredee watched, the gawky youth paled, stammered and then stumbled away from Lady Phoebe, who turned to her brother, mouth drawn in a tight little bow.

"What did he want?" Mrs. Price begged, hurrying up to Meredee, breaths coming in little pants. "Does he suspect?"

Meredee shook her head. "No. He talked only of science and philosophy."

"Science?" Her stepmother drew a breath that swelled her lacy bodice. "I would not have thought him capable of it."

Across the room, the earl took his sister's arm and drew her toward the door that led to the wells. "Just because he's taken a dislike to Algernon," Meredee said, "doesn't make him a monster, madam."

"Well, I like that!" Mrs. Price huffed. "And why was I dragged from my home if not to escape a monster?"

Meredee sighed and took her arm. "I begin to wonder. Have you drunk from the wells, then?"

"No," her stepmother said with a pout. "I didn't

dare leave the room once I saw you conversing with that wretch."

"Then let's get you a cup." She led her stepmother through the long room and out the door.

Once outside, the sound of the waves came louder. At high tide, she knew, they could pound against the rounded stones of the terrace and dampen the path with spray. Now a few leaves dotted the dark steps as they made their way down to the stone-lined recess that housed the two wells. Mrs. Price was convinced the Chalybeate Well was the finer of the two, so Meredee steered her toward the line of people waiting for a drink dipped from the stone-edged hole of the south well by a gentle widow.

One of the wonders of Scarborough was the variety of people who were welcomed at the wells. Everyone from Mrs. Price's new friend, the countess, to the tiny son of the local coalmonger stood waiting their turns, sure that a sip from the mineral springs would make them stronger, or at least more fashionable. But Meredee and Mrs. Price had only taken a few steps when she saw Lord Allyndale and Lady Phoebe near the north well.

Mrs. Price must have sighted him at nearly the same time, for she nudged Meredee. "Smile," she hissed. "You do not want him to think anything's amiss."

Meredee forced a smile, but neither of the Dearborns seemed to be looking in her direction. They had reached the front of their line and stood beside the low well. Mrs. Dennings, one of the elderly widows who served the water, lifted a tin cup. Meredee thought that surely Lady Phoebe would take it, but she refused the spa water with a shake of her honey-colored curls and a scrunch of her pert nose. To Meredee's surprise, it was the earl who drank of the healing waters, head up, gaze out over the sea, in one great gulp as if taking particularly foul medicine.

Her father had drunk it like that, when he was afraid of dying.

Meredee blinked. Chase Dearborn could not be ill. Her father had been thin and growing thinner every day, his skin gray, his eyes shadowed. Lord Allyndale looked the picture of health—tall, solid, imposing. He turned and saw her staring at him then, and her cheeks heated in a blush.

For a moment, their gazes locked, held. Why did he look at her so intently? Did he find her as intriguing to watch? Had he found their conversation as interesting as she had? Did he admire her?

The stone floor seemed to shift under her. She caught her breath and clutched her stepmother's arm to hold herself steady. Lord Allyndale merely inclined his head in acknowledgement, then walked swiftly to the stairs, his sister hurrying behind.

"Well, I like that!" Mrs. Price grumbled, her gaze following them. "Not even a fare thee well!" She paled suddenly and grabbed Meredee's hand where it still rested on her arm. "Did you say something to make him take us in dislike?"

Meredee took a deep breath and pulled away. What was wrong with her? Had she expected some kind of public display? She wasn't the type to inspire sonnets; by his own admission he wasn't the type to compose them. If she hadn't saved his sister's life, they would probably have never met.

"I don't believe his actions had anything to do with us," she told her stepmother.

Mrs. Price nodded, biting her lower lip. But Meredee couldn't tell her what she really thought, for surely that was an even greater fancy. If she hadn't known better, she would have thought the earl was running away from her, just as she'd run from him the other day.

"But wasn't that Miss Price?" Phoebe asked as Chase all but stuffed her into their waiting carriage outside the spa house.

"It was, but I spoke to her earlier." He climbed in beside her, shut the door and rapped on the upper panel to signal his driver to start. He hadn't intended to talk to Meredee Price, though he'd noticed her the moment he'd entered the spa. Something about her drew his attention, awakened his senses. He'd have liked nothing better than to spend a few hours in her company. But he knew he had to be circumspect. Undue attentions usually led to assumptions of betrothals he had no intention of confirming. He hadn't come to Scarborough looking for a wife. Only his life.

Phoebe tossed her head. "Well, I didn't get to speak to her. You might have asked before whisking me off."

"You'll see her tonight, pet," he reminded her. "And, if I know you, you have a great deal to do to get ready for dinner."

Phoebe's pique eased at that, and she prattled on about hair and gowns for the quarter hour it took to reach their Scarborough house above the spa. Chase was just as glad. Phoebe had been away at school when he'd first fallen ill. She didn't know the fevers that racked him with no warning, leaving him weak, helpless.

The London physicians blamed it on humors in the blood; the renowned physician he'd consulted in Edinburgh was certain it had to do with the night air on the York moors. *Mal aria,* the Italians called it. Either way, he was determined to rid himself of the malady. His sister and his duties as earl required him to be alert, focused, dedicated. Falling into a stupor for days at a time was simply not an option.

If only he could find Phoebe a suitable husband, but the girl seemed drawn to feckless fools—all charm, no substance. He did not doubt for an instant that they would prove weak reeds in times of trouble.

Given Chase's illness, Phoebe had to have someone at her side she could count on.

Unbidden, Meredee Price's face came to mind. She never ceased to amaze him. What other woman in his circles had ever been interested in science, could actually converse knowledgeably about the subject? Moreover, she had a way of looking at him that made him feel as if she could see deep inside. For a moment, at the spa, he was certain she'd divined his secret, that taking the waters wasn't simply a show of being fashionable but a desperate attempt to cure himself. Yet instead of ridicule he saw in her face, it was compassion.

"Allyndale, you are not paying attention," Phoebe complained, forcing him back to the present. "I asked you a very important question."

Chase inclined his head. "Forgive me. What do you need?"

Phoebe leaned forward, dark eyes narrowed. "Shall I wear pearls or roses in my hair tonight?"

Chase's chuckle came out before he could catch it. "You will be delightful in either, my dear."

She cocked her head. "You like Miss Price, don't you?"

Oh, he was entirely too transparent. He schooled his face into something significantly more stern, a look that made his servants tiptoe about the house and Parliament tremble. "That, young miss, is none of your affair."

Phoebe let out a peal of laughter. "Oh, you do, you do! How delightful! I've been praying so long for the right woman for you. I can't believe I've found a sister at last!"

"Your felicitations are entirely premature, I assure you."

"So you say, but time will tell. And when you are happy, perhaps you'll be willing to let me be happy too."

Her words knifed him. "Are you so very unhappy, Phoebe? I thought you wanted to come to Scarborough."

She dropped her gaze and fiddled with the bow on her fetching bonnet. "I did. It isn't Scarborough that makes me so unhappy. I miss him, Chase. I told you I would."

Chase's pulse pounded in his temples. "He isn't worthy of you, Phoebe. You know that."

"You know that," she said with a sigh. "My heart never agreed with you."

"Then perhaps it's time you spoke to your heart," Chase said, feeling his tightening inside him. "A marriage should be well thought out, the people well known to each other. You cannot fall in love in an instant and expect to have made a good choice."

She raised her gaze to his, her dark eyes stormy. "Oh, I hope you fall in love, so swiftly and suddenly that nothing else matters! Perhaps then you'll understand how I feel!"

She had no idea what she asked. Chase turned away from her before harsh words came out. He had no intention of falling in love, swiftly or otherwise. No amount of love had kept Phoebe safe before. That was where his duty lay. And nothing she or the lovely Miss Price could say would change that.

Chapter Four

Meredee knew she ought to be quivering in her slippers that she was going to dine with Lord Allyndale. At the very least she should be plotting stratagems to get him to confess all. But when she was with him, she found herself talking instead.

How could she not admire a man who wasn't afraid to share his thoughts about science and philosophy, who seemed to genuinely enjoy her company? He was a refreshing change from the gentlemen her stepmother entertained. They lived at the very surface of life, talking in generalities. Algernon's friends were worse. To them, she was an antidote—the poor spinster to be pitied. She hadn't realized until this morning how much she craved more.

A salt-tanged wind was blowing in from the sea as she and Mrs. Price alighted from their carriage in front of the Dearborn house. The moist air brushed the carefully arranged curls at the sides of Meredee's face. A tingle of excitement shot through her. A sea breeze in the evening often meant a storm was brewing. She might be able to go hunting in the morning! But before she could do more than think about what that would mean to her promise to her father, her gaze lit on the house, and all other thoughts fled.

Most of the people who flocked to Scarborough stayed in lodging houses or inns. A few rented a house overlooking the spa. Lord Allyndale's house was of square rosy stone, three stories tall, with fluted columns across the front that softened the imposing lines. Candlelight glowed from every multipaned window, casting shadows across the stone steps. Meredee was glad she'd worn her best evening gown, a buttercup-yellow satin, striped with bands of delicate gold embroidery from the square bodice to the narrow hem.

Before she could take more than two steps, the front door opened, and Lady Phoebe rushed down the stairs to enfold Meredee in her arms. "Oh, you've come, you've come!"

Meredee managed to disengage with a smile. "Well, it truly isn't difficult to travel the half mile unscathed."

Lady Phoebe linked her arm with Meredee's and drew her up the stairs and into the house, leaving Mrs. Price to pick up her amethyst-colored skirts and trail behind. The inside of the house was even more grand than the outside. The entry hall was tiled in black-and-white marble, the pale blue walls edged in white leaves and graced with landscape paintings of rolling hills and stormy skies.

"What a lovely home," Meredee murmured.

"It isn't ours," Lady Phoebe explained, bouncing on her pink kid slippers. The girl was dressed as usual in a becoming shade of pink, her gown boasting no less than three rows of flouncing at the generous hem. "We didn't even get to bring our favorite paintings or furnishings."

"You didn't get to bring *your* favorites, you mean," her brother corrected her, descending the graceful curving stair. "I have an aversion to living in pink."

Tonight he was impeccable in black, from his tailored coat to the breeches, black satin-striped waistcoat, and patent shoes. The dark color made the white of his shirt and simply tied cravat blaze against his skin and the gold of his hair. He bowed over their hands, and Meredee curtsied, mouth suddenly dry.

"We are expecting one more guest," he said as he released her. "Allow me to escort you to the drawing room to wait."

Mrs. Price tittered a reply and accepted his offered arm. Meredee and Lady Phoebe fell into step behind them. The girl squeezed her arm. "I'm so glad you could join us," she said, as if her glowing face and bright smile could have given Meredee any doubt. "I think my brother is smitten with you."

Meredee missed a step and nearly trod on her hem.

"Oh, Lady Phoebe," she whispered. "You mustn't say such things."

"Why not?" Lady Phoebe peered over at her, suddenly serious. "Most women find my brother irresistible. Don't you?"

Meredee eyed his back, so imposing in the tailored coat. His hair was just long enough that wisps brushed the high collar as he walked. How could a man who was known to be so hard have such soft-looking hair? "I hardly know your brother," she said aloud, cheeks blazing, "so I'm sure I'm in no position to say."

Lady Phoebe gave her arm another squeeze as they reached the drawing room. "Then perhaps you can become better acquainted."

"Perhaps," Meredee answered, though she was beginning to believe that the most important thing she could do was to determine who exactly Chase Dearborn, Earl of Allyndale, was.

Yet try as she might, she simply could not find the monster Algernon insisted on. Lord Allyndale made polite conversation with her stepmother, his face set in firm lines that said he was listening to every bit of nonsense as if to a speech on an important issue in Parliament. He gave equal attention to his sister's meandering story about shopping for a new pair of gloves. His patience would have been endearing, if Meredee could forget the scowl he'd worn that afternoon at the spa that had made the tall youth flee as if in fear for his life.

Had he looked at Algernon that way? Would he look at her that way if he knew she was Algernon's stepsister?

"Still so unhappy?" he ventured when Lady Phoebe had drawn Mrs. Price over to the spinet to show her some new sheet music. "Do you find Scarborough such a sad place, Miss Price?"

She could not give him her thoughts. "A little," she admitted instead. "My father brought me here every summer. I haven't been back since he died. It doesn't feel the same."

"I am sorry for your loss," he said quietly.

She could not stand his kindness. "I'll see him again someday. Until then, there is much to interest me."

"Such as?"

She glanced up at him. There was that look again, head cocked, blue eyes dark and serious, as if what she had to say was critical to his very existence. The look made her want to be brilliant, if only to gratify his attention. "Good company, new music, the sun on the waves." She grinned. "And there are always the improving works of Hannah More."

"Or Mary Wollstonecraft," he agreed with a matching grin.

The butler coughed from the doorway, and everyone looked up. "Sir Trevor Fitzwilliam has arrived, ladies, my lord."

Meredee held her smile from long practice, but

Lady Phoebe gasped as if she hadn't seen him in years and rushed to tug him into the room. "Oh, Trevor, come meet Miss Meredee Price. She saved my life."

"A pleasure to see you again, Miss Price," he said with a bow. "And this must be your lovely sister."

"Very nearly." Mrs. Price beamed as she joined the group.

"Again?" Lady Phoebe interrupted with a frown. "You said it was a pleasure to see her again. Do you know her?"

Meredee glanced at Lord Allyndale. Surely it was his place to explain their meeting yesterday afternoon to his sister. She only wondered why he hadn't done so sooner. The faintest of pinks tinged his cheeks, as if he'd been caught in an indiscretion. "Sir Trevor and I stopped by the Bell Inn yesterday," he said to his sister. "Just to be certain Miss Price had not taken ill from her efforts on your behalf."

"But why should she take ill?" Lady Phoebe persisted. "I was the one in need of rescue."

"Ah," her brother said, looking over her head, "there's Beagan again. Dinner is apparently ready. Shall we, ladies?" He offered his arm to Meredee. Her surprise must have shown on her face, for he smiled. "You are the guest of honor, are you not? The savior of Scarborough Bay, I believe I heard."

"Nothing of the sort," Meredee said, wishing Mrs. Murdock had never coined the phrase. But she set her hand on his arm nonetheless and was surprised to feel a tension matching her own. What could possibly have discomposed the earl? Had he come to the inn for some other purpose?

"And I am the lucky one," Sir Trevor said, offering one arm to Lady Phoebe and the other to Mrs. Price. "I have the pleasure of escorting two beauties to dinner."

Phoebe's giggle was nearly eclipsed by Mrs. Price's.

The dining room was long and high, with the same pale blue walls edged in white and the ceiling painted with puffy clouds and pink-cheeked cherubs. Lord Allyndale led her to a gilded chair on his left, while Lady Phoebe took up the chair at his right and Mrs. Price sat beside the girl, leaving Sir Trevor to sit on Meredee's other side.

Meredee was spared conversation as footmen brought in a tureen of steaming onion soup, platters of roast beef and salmon, and plates of buttered prawns, fresh asparagus and broccoli. She was a little surprised when Lord Allyndale did not ask her or his sister which dishes they preferred but filled their plates with what must have appealed to him.

"Is the beef not to your liking?" he asked her when she had stared down at the loaded gold-rimmed china for a few moments.

Meredee glanced up at him. "I'm sure it's delicious, my lord. I would love to try the salmon, too."

He blinked as if it had never dawned on him she

might have a specific preference. "Certainly. Trevor, be a good man and find room on Miss Price's place for the fish."

Meredee turned to the baronet before he could reach for the plate. "If you'd be so good as to pass the plate my way, Sir Trevor, I'm certain I can serve myself."

"Your servant, Miss Price," he assured her.

She was thankful when Lady Phoebe monopolized the conversation for most of the first course. She had to find a way to ask the earl why he'd come to Scarborough. But every gambit seemed too obvious, too calculated. She glanced his way several times, and each time he smiled as if in encouragement. Yet she couldn't seem to bring the words to her lips.

"Miss Price was telling me her theories on the earth's magnetic fields," the earl put in at one point.

Lady Phoebe blinked as if, for once, she could find nothing to say on the topic. Sir Trevor dug more deeply into his asparagus as if searching for hidden treasure.

"I'm certain you would know far more, my lord," Mrs. Price said with a warning look to Meredee. "No one in my household could lay claim to being a bluestocking." She laughed as if the very notion was absurd.

"Interesting," he replied with a smile. "I've always found the study of scientific topics to be commendable, in either sex."

"Well, well, certainly," Mrs. Price stammered. "Might I have some more of that delightful salmon, my lord? I must have the recipe for my cook."

Chase passed her the plate. As he returned to his meal, his left eyelid drifted closed for a second. Heavens, had he just winked at her?

The second course was even more elaborate, with herbed pheasant, sole smothered in mushrooms, a ragout of celery, tart apple pie, sweet trifle and strawberry ice cream in a silver bucket. This time, she noticed, Lord Allyndale made certain to pass each dish to her for her choice, his hands firm on the fine china. Yet she couldn't help wondering whether they would hold a pistol so steadily if it were aimed at her stepbrother's heart.

"Still not to your liking?" he murmured. "You have the most determined frown on your face."

Meredee forced her lips upward. "I have never had so many wonderful dishes, my lord."

He nodded as if satisfied. "I'll be sure to pass your compliment on to Mrs. Downthistle."

So he took the trouble to praise his staff, and he knew their names. Her father, God rest his soul, had found it more convenient to call them by their purpose—Cook or Coachman.

Determined not to wait another minute, she set her fork down. "What brought you to Scarborough, my lord?" she asked.

Mrs. Price, who had been drawn into an animated

conversation with Lady Phoebe, broke off in midsentence to listen to his answer. Even Sir Trevor paused, fork halfway to his mouth. Lord Allyndale must have noticed he was suddenly the focus of every eye, because he raised his brows.

"There's no great secret," he said. "I dislike London summers. Scarborough is close enough to our estate to be both a distraction and a convenience."

Lady Phoebe made a face. "He means he can hurry home whenever he likes." She shook her finger at him. "You lack all spirit of adventure!"

His chuckle made Meredee smile. "Perhaps I do have a preference for my own fire."

"And what of you, Miss Price?" Sir Trevor asked on her left. "What brings you and your sister to Scarborough?"

Mrs. Price batted her lashes and answered for Meredee. "Why, to be entertained by young scamps like you, sir."

Sir Trevor smiled at her sally but turned his attention immediately back to Meredee. As Lord Allyndale offered to refill her stepmother's plate, his friend lowered his voice. "And are you also here for the company, Miss Price?"

Those green eyes were far too watchful. "I go wherever my stepmother needs me, sir."

"Ah, then you were not left with an independence."

How rude! Did he think to win an heiress with so

bold a question? She frowned at him, but her eyes were drawn to the stickpin in his snowy cravat. It gleamed dully, as if the diamond had been exchanged with paste. And surely those stitches at the lapel of his coat indicated where it had been skillfully patched. The baronet, it seemed, had to economize. Small wonder finances were of such interest to him.

"No," she said. "My father left me no dowry."

"A shame," he replied. "I don't believe I'm familiar with your father or the Price family. Where are you from?"

Why did he persist? He could not be interested in her. His financial circumstances would demand a wealthy bride. And his pride would likely demand a beautiful one.

"Are you a student of genealogy, Sir Trevor?" she asked, taking up her fork and spearing the sole.

He blinked. "I beg your pardon?"

"Genealogy, the study of one's antecedents. You seem keenly interested in mine. Is it your hobby?"

His mouth opened and closed, as if he could not find the wit to respond.

"Many gentlemen have hobbies," she offered, taking pity on him. "You may have seen Colonel Williams at the spa—tall fellow, favors his right leg—he studies rocks. Mr. Cranell, who you may have seen partnering my stepmother at cards, deciphers the meaning and origin of names. My father collected seashells."

"How delightful," he said, managing to sound anything but delighted. "And what do you collect, Miss Price?"

"Apparently, gentlemen intent on quizzing me," she replied.

"More sole, Miss Price?" Lord Allyndale put in, forcing her to turn away from Sir Trevor before the baronet could formulate a reply. Lord Allyndale's mouth was held in a tight line as he offered her the plate, but his blue eyes twinkled. He was obviously trying not to laugh.

But was it Sir Trevor or her who had amused him?

What a cipher Miss Price was. She smiled readily at quips, responded appropriately to most questions. She was the picture of loveliness, all shades of gold, sitting beside him. But when she thought no one was watching, her face betrayed her least emotion. At moments, he caught her gazing at him with such perplexity that he wondered what she was seeing.

"She has no money, no family to brag of and a cutting wit," Trevor said after the ladies had left them to their conversation. "I see no need to prolong the acquaintance."

Chase shook his head. "Is that all you noticed? She has a admirable presence, a commendable loyalty and an enviable intelligence."

"Yes, and strength and vitality. By all means hire

her as your sister's companion, but look for more in a wife."

"What makes you think I'm looking for a wife?" Chase asked with a laugh.

"Miss Price is obviously no danger," Trevor replied. "Why else show such interest?" He moved from his chair to the one Meredee had vacated and leaned closer. "Listen—I had word from a friend today. That's why I was detained. Delacorte is back in London."

Chase snorted. "His creditors will no doubt be delighted to hear it."

"But you should not. It seems he blames you for his troubles, or so he confided over too much wine. He claims Phoebe loves him, and you forced them apart."

Chase felt his mouth tighten. "He has no right to speak of Phoebe, not after trying to force her into marriage."

"Agreed. I only tell you to warn you."

Chase nodded. "And I appreciate that. I promise you, I won't allow the man to hurt my sister."

But Phoebe would not make his job any easier, Chase thought as he and Trevor went to join the ladies in the withdrawing room. His sister seemed stuck in perpetual girlhood, always focused on her own needs. He'd never told her about Victor Delacorte's plan to abduct her and force her to marry him. Chase and Trev had stopped him before he could carry through with his plans, and Chase had decided not to explain it all to Phoebe, concerned he might frighten her into a shell. But would she act any more sensibly if Delacorte showed his face again?

Chapter Five

When Chase and Trevor entered the withdrawing room, Phoebe was playing at the spinet while Meredee and her stepmother sat on dainty chairs, listening. Trevor immediately went to turn pages for Phoebe. Chase joined his other guests.

"Your sister is an impassioned player, my lord," Meredee ventured, her gaze on Phoebe's flying fingers.

"My sister seldom does anything without passion," Chase replied. "Do you play, Miss Price?"

"No. My father thought it more important that I memorize the Latin names of seashells than to learn to play. I sing on occasion."

She said it without rancor, but the way she continued to watch his sister told him she wondered what it would have been like had it been otherwise.

"Perhaps you would care to share a song with us," he suggested.

Her gaze did not waver, though her cheeks reddened. "I'm sure you would much rather listen to your sister."

Something in her tone indicated that she'd far prefer to listen. Yet the more he knew of her, the less he believed that she was shy and retiring. She spoke her mind easily enough. Why not sing? Most women he knew loved performing.

"We cannot require our kind host and hostess to furnish all the entertainment," her stepmother put in. "I'm sure you would not want Lord Allyndale to take us in dislike."

She paled at that, as if losing his good regard meant the noose. Was it her stepmother who was pushing her at him then? He'd certainly met a few marriage-minded mamas since he'd ascended to his title.

He leaned closer to Meredee and caught the scent of lavender from her golden hair. "My sister adores being the center of attention. Sing only if it amuses you, Miss Price."

She met his gaze, her gray eyes dark and unfathomable. Once again he had the impression that she could see deep inside him, knew every thought in his head. This time he found it far more intriguing.

"Thank you for your kind offer, my lord," she murmured. "If you'd like, I'll sing."

He felt the oddest urge to reach out and press her hand in thanks. Instead, he rose and called to his sister. "Miss Price has agreed to favor us with a song."

Phoebe immediately stopped playing and clapped her hands. "Splendid! Let's see what we both know."

Meredee rose to join her, and the two conferred a moment, Meredee's golden crown near Phoebe's darker blond curls. They settled on a song quickly, agreed on the key, and Phoebe played an introduction. Chase took a seat beside Mrs. Price.

Meredee's voice was high and sweet, the song encouraging. He felt himself leaning forward, nodding along. She kept her gaze focused in the distance, as if unaware of her rapt audience, every part of her tuned to her task. Funny, he'd always wondered how angels would sing. Perhaps now he knew.

Meredee's heart was pounding so loudly she wondered that anyone had heard a word she'd sung. Yet there was Lord Allyndale, smiling at her as if she'd discovered the way to reach the moon. She wanted to bathe in the glow, drink deeply of his pleasure. But, as she finished, his butler coughed behind him, and he rose to go speak with the fellow in low tones. Sir Trevor joined them.

"Very nice," Lady Phoebe said, closing the sheet music. Meredee nodded and wandered back to her stepmother. She hadn't noticed that the room was so dark. It had seemed much brighter when the earl was smiling at her.

Lord Allyndale returned to their sides and eyed Meredee and her stepmother. Gone was the smile, to be replaced by a frown that sent a shiver through her. "I'm afraid I have bad news. I cannot allow either of you to leave this house tonight."

Meredee gasped. Did he know? Had someone sent word that Algernon was in Scarborough? Had she somehow given them away by singing her stepbrother's favorite song?

Mrs. Price rose shakily to her feet. "Stay here? Why?"

"I'm told a storm has sprung up," he replied. "Between Phoebe's playing and our location at the back of the house, we didn't notice." He paused a moment, and Meredee knew she wasn't the only one listening. Now she heard it, an uneven rising and falling, as if harsh winds drove pouring rain this way and that.

"Oh," Mrs. Price said, sinking back onto her seat with a strained laugh. "A storm. Of course."

"My lord, we cannot impose," Meredee started, but the earl held up his hand.

"And I cannot be responsible for turning my guests or my staff out into this deluge. You and your coachman will spend the night here. I'm sure the inn will hold your rooms."

"Well certainly, but …" Mrs. Price trailed off and looked helplessly at Meredee.

She was fairly sure she knew her stepmother's concern. Algernon would be waiting to hear what they'd learned about Lord Allyndale's purpose in Scarborough. When they didn't return, what would her stepbrother do?

"It's settled then," Lord Allyndale said. "If you'll excuse me, I'll instruct the staff to arrange rooms for the three of you." As if their agreement was never in question, he strode from the room. Sir Trevor also excused himself to check on his horse.

In short order, Meredee found herself ensconced in an elegant bedchamber. She was surprised that Lady Phoebe hadn't chosen it for herself, for the walls were a pale pink edged in white like the inside of one of her father's shells, and the furniture was rosewood with gold appointments. A cheery fire was already burning in the white marble fireplace. How lovely it would be to sink into the thick mattress, snuggle under the pretty coverlet. Yet was it advisable to stay?

She pulled aside the heavy crimson drapes and peered out into a dark night where darker shapes of trees whipped back and forth, and rain pattered on the glass. Staying indoors was definitely safer. If only she could be certain Algernon would do the same!

She wasn't sure what she was to do about toiletries and sleeping attire, but a harried young maid brought her an ivory-backed brush and comb and a lace-edged white flannel nightgown that smelled faintly of camphor.

"Retrieved from a chest in the attic, miss," the girl confided as she helped Meredee out of her corset and into the soft folds of the flannel. "The other lady was small enough to wear one of Lady Phoebe's things, but you're built on entirely different lines, if I may be so free."

Meredee was just thankful to have something to wear and told the girl so, then dismissed her so the maid could return to Lady Phoebe. Meredee was sitting in one of the chairs by the fire, combing out her hair, when there was a tap at her door.

"It's Phoebe," said a whispered voice when Meredee asked who it was. "May I come in?"

Meredee hurried to open the paneled door for her, and the girl slipped into the room, her filmy white nightgown trailing behind her like wisps of fog.

"Are you all settled?" she asked with a smile undimmed by the lateness of the hour or the circumstances. "My brother wanted to make sure everything was to your liking. I told him to come ask you himself. I think I scandalized the poor dear."

"You scandalize me, Lady Phoebe," Meredee said, but she couldn't help smiling at the girl's giggle.

Lady Phoebe took both of Meredee's hands. "I just knew we were going to be friends. May I call you Meredee?"

"Of course," Meredee replied, touched by the intimacy.

The girl pulled her to the bed and crawled up onto the creamy quilted bedcover. "And now we can have a nice coz."

"Now?" Meredee stood beside the bed with a frown.

Phoebe spread her hands. "Of course now! That's why one has friends stay over—to whisper confidences long into the night."

"I sincerely doubt that's what your brother had in mind."

"Probably not," Phoebe agreed. "But it's what I had in mind from the moment he suggested that you stay." She flopped back onto the covers and gazed up at the rosy brocaded hangings that draped the canopied bed. "I've always wanted a sister." She popped up on her elbows. "Do you have any family, Meredee?"

Meredee perched on the edge of the bed. Lady Phoebe was so open, so giving. She hated having to lie. "No sisters, I'm afraid," she said.

Phoebe sighed. "Well, I suppose brothers have their uses. Sometimes."

"You're doing it too brown," Meredee said. "Your brother seems devoted to you."

Phoebe plummeted onto her back again. "Oh, he is. Perhaps too devoted."

Meredee lay back as well and gazed over at the girl, whose honey-colored curls had fanned out on the coverlet. "I haven't felt like part of a family since my father died. Even then he was fairly busy with his own activities. I think having someone looking out for you would be wonderful. Is there such a thing as too much devotion?"

"There is if it smothers you."

Meredee frowned. "What do you mean?"

Phoebe sighed. "It's like he doesn't trust me, like he cannot believe I might have an idea counter to his." She waved a hand. "This whole 'You will stay the night' thing is a perfect example. He never asked your permission, he never so much as asked your opinion. He decided you'd stay, and that was that."

Just as he'd filled her plate at dinner, Meredee realized. "But his request was reasonable," she couldn't help pointing out. "His decision was made with our best interests at heart."

"All Chase's decisions are made with the very best of intentions," Phoebe assured her. "That doesn't make them right. If I had my way, I'd never have left London."

Meredee's pulse quickened. She'd thought to question Lord Allyndale, and here was his sister ready to tell her all. Yet how could she take advantage of Lady Phoebe's generous spirit?

Lord, show me how to be a friend to her.

"Why did you leave, then?" Meredee asked.

Phoebe's hand slapped down on the covers. "Because Chase insisted on it!"

Meredee nodded. "Yes, I understand that. But why? I've never heard your names in Scarborough before, so it obviously isn't your usual summer haunt. You had to rent a house; you didn't get to set it up the way you liked. You must have left in a hurry."

"Oh, a terrible rush! I didn't even have a chance to tell most of my friends I was leaving."

"But why?" Meredee pressed.

Phoebe smoothed the coverlet she'd wrinkled with her slap only a moment before. "You won't think badly of me, will you, Miss Price?"

Heavens, what had she uncovered? Had Lady Phoebe committed some scandal? The girl was so impetuous, Meredee could well imagine her tumbling into something before she thought better of it. *Lord, give me guidance.* "I'm sure you've noticed that I think quite highly of you, Lady Phoebe," she said gently. "And I believe I was to be Meredee."

Phoebe's smile was tremulous. "So you are, my dear Meredee." She scooted a little closer and lowered her voice, as if to keep even the storm from hearing. "We left London," she whispered, dark eyes intent on Meredee's face, "because I fell in love."

Meredee sucked in a breath. "And your brother disapproved?"

Phoebe nodded vigorously, squashing her curls against the covers. "Assuredly! He insists that my beau is completely beneath me. But I don't care! I'll find a way. Love cannot be denied!"

Her voice was rising again, and this time it was Meredee who caught her hand and motioned her with the other to calm herself. "Think about what you're saying. Your brother loves you, and he's obviously intelligent. If he disliked this young man, he may well have had reason."

Phoebe shook her head. "No reason that I can see."

"Is he of good family? Can he support you? Is he of good Christian character?"

"Yes, yes, yes!" Phoebe exclaimed. "And he is handsome and charming and makes me laugh."

There could be worse things, Meredee thought. "And does he share your desire to marry?"

Phoebe sighed. "Yes. Perhaps. I think so." She sat up. "Oh, don't you see? I'll never have a chance to find out. And it's all my brother's fault!"

Someone rapped on the door.

Phoebe shrank against the headboard as if defeated. "Oh, pooh! That must be Chase. He's found me."

"You are not an escaped prisoner," Meredee reminded her in a whisper. "I'm certain no one will mind if you come bid me good-night."

The rap came again, louder. "Miss Price?" Lord Allyndale's voice was unmistakable. "I'm sorry to trouble you. May I have a word?"

Phoebe clutched her arm. "Please don't make me leave. I want to stay, with you."

Was that fear in Lady Phoebe's puckered face? Was her brother so cruel, then? Meredee knew she ought to be glad she'd learned the truth, yet she didn't want it to be true. She found his company, his smile, his admiration irresistible. She didn't want him to be anything less than a man she could admire, too.

But once again, Lady Phoebe's eyes were large and beseeching. And just as when she'd seen the girl struggling in the sea, Meredee knew she couldn't ignore her worries. She patted Phoebe's hand and pulled away.

"Coming!" she called toward the door. Then, to Phoebe, "I'll only be a moment. Don't be afraid. I won't let any harm come to you."

She thought the girl might protest, but Lady Phoebe merely bit her lip and nodded. Pulling a spare blanket from the foot of the bed, Meredee draped its warmth around her shoulders and padded to the door.

She opened it just wide enough to peer out, but the sight before her made her breath catch. Chase Dearborn had discarded his black coat and now stood in shirtsleeves and waistcoat. The linen draped his broad shoulders; the waistcoat emphasized the solid line of him. Another time he might have looked commanding, but his cravat was carelessly tied and rumpled as if he'd retied it in a hurry, and his blue eyes were every bit as wide as Phoebe's.

He ran a hand back through his hair, disheveling the sandy locks. "Forgive the interruption. It's my habit to look in on my sister before I retire. She doesn't appear to be in her room. Have you seen her?"

She thought she heard a faint rustle behind her,

as if Phoebe had pulled the covers over her head to hide. Was she so concerned about getting caught out of bed? Surely she was too old for strict bedtimes. And Chase did not seem intent on enforcing one. The lines bracketing his eyes and mouth told her he was sincerely worried.

But what if she was wrong? What if the pleasure of his company had blinded her to his faults? What if he truly was so cruel as to dominate his own sister?

"Is she given to wandering away, my lord?" she tried. "Perhaps she only sought a book to read before retiring."

Even his chuckle sounded strained. "Unlike you, Phoebe is not given to much reading. If she isn't in her room, there's something afoot, you may depend upon it."

"But where could she go in a storm?" Meredee protested.

He paled as if just imagining made him ill. "You might be surprised. Forgive me for troubling you. Sleep well." He turned from the door, and Meredee could almost see the weight that pressed him down. She did not think he would sleep at all at this rate. She reached out a hand and snagged the back of his waistcoat, her fingers brushing the muscle in his back. "My lord, wait." When he turned with a frown, she lowered her voice and her hand. "I do not like betraying a confidence, but your sister is here, with me. We were chatting before retiring."

She had the satisfaction in seeing his shoulders slump as if she had relieved a burden.

"Thank you," he said, straightening. "Now if you would just send her out to me, I have a few words for her before she retires."

It was an order, not a request, just as Phoebe had predicted. Did his sister really need him to keep such a close watch on her? Who did he think was a danger? His friend, Sir Trevor? Mrs. Price?

Or Meredee?

Chapter Six

The storm blew itself out sometime in the middle of
the night, and Chase woke to a world washed clean.
His own mood was surprisingly light as Valcom, his
valet, shaved him and helped him dress for the day.
A good ride along the hills above town—that's what
he needed: fresh air, quiet, an unobstructed view. He
had no urgent estate business. Phoebe was his only
concern, and, if he knew his sister, she wouldn't rise
before noon. He could not imagine his unexpected
guests would do otherwise. He had all morning to
himself.

"If Miss Price or her stepmother come down to eat
before I return," he told Beagan over breakfast, "ask
them to wait."

The butler cleared his throat. For a butler, Beagan
was rather short, coming only to Chase's chin. He also
had a slow, considerate voice and a walk to match.
But the set to his rounded face, the stiffness in his

bearing, brooked no nonsense. "I'm afraid Miss Price has already gone, my lord."

Chase frowned. "Gone? But the sun can't have been up over an hour."

"She came down to the kitchens before the sun rose." His wrinkled face showed how scandalized he was by this unorthodox behavior. "She thanked the staff for our service, asked to be remembered to you and Lady Phoebe and took herself off."

"On foot?" When Beagan nodded, Chase tossed down his napkin and rose. "Have my horse saddled and out front in five minutes."

His butler's steps were considerably faster than usual as he hurried to comply.

What was wrong with the woman, traipsing about the streets in the early morning hours? Who knew what kind of ruffian she'd meet! Had she no thought for her own safety? What was so urgent that it would require her attention? He considered rousing her stepmother and demanding an explanation but decided against it. If Mrs. Price knew something personal, she was unlikely to confide in Chase. If she didn't know the reason for her stepdaughter's sudden departure, he'd only worry her.

Five minutes later, he was riding down the drive, good mood flown with his freedom. Wasn't it just like a society miss to act so fecklessly, with no thought about how it might affect others? Small wonder he had to watch out for Phoebe at every turn. Miss Price obviously needed just such a protector.

He realized that he'd urged his horse into a canter and slowed the bay to a walk. When had Meredee Price become his responsibility to protect? He was no relation, and he had no claim to her affections. He wasn't even sure he wanted such a claim. At times, she seemed more intelligent and sensible than most of the women he'd known. But until he knew Phoebe was settled and his own affliction had been dealt with, he was in no position to offer a lady anything. It was only, he told himself, that Miss Price had been a guest under his roof that drove him to ensure her safety now.

He rode into the coaching yard of the Bell Inn and dismounted, tossing his reins to a waiting stable boy. Of the inn's inhabitants, few were stirring so early in the morning. A young maid was poking up the fire in the great hearth, and two older gentlemen were nursing cups of steaming tea by the front window. Chase caught a glimpse of a slight, dark-haired young man heading up the stairs. At the sound of Chase's boots on the floor, the fellow turned, and Chase started.

Algernon Whitaker? Here?

The man scurried up the stairs before Chase could be sure. He shook himself. It couldn't be Whitaker. He very much doubted the fellow rose any earlier than Phoebe. And he'd certainly never show himself in his shirtsleeves in the common room of an inn, especially in anything so mundane as pale linen. Algernon Whitaker favored bright yellows and lurid reds. Chase shuddered just remembering.

No, Whitaker couldn't be in Scarborough. Chase was just so used to seeing villains in the shadows that he now saw them in the early morning light. The fact disgusted him.

"My lord," the innkeeper exclaimed, hurrying in from the kitchens and bowing low. A gentleman of ample proportions and neat appearance, he wore a wide smile, his bald head gleaming. "An unexpected pleasure! How may I serve you?"

"I'm concerned about one of your guests," Chase explained. "Miss Meredee Price. She and her stepmother stayed with my sister and me last night in the storm, but I understand from my staff that she left at dawn. Has she returned?"

"Returned and gone," the innkeeper proclaimed.

Chase frowned at him. "Gone? Gone where?"

The innkeeper chuckled. "You must not have known Miss Meredee long, my lord. She's gone where all Prices go after a storm—to the shore."

He knew his frown was growing, for the innkeeper's smile faded. "To the shore?" Chase asked. "Why?"

Servants and merchants usually catered to his least desire, but the innkeeper's round face tightened up like a miser's purse. "I'm sure you'll have to ask the lady, my lord, seeing as how she didn't see fit to confide in you herself." He nodded to the door. "Very likely she's crossed half the South Bay by now. If you hurry, you may catch her before the tide turns."

Meredee Price certainly commanded loyalties, Chase thought as he nodded his thanks and strode out to his waiting horse. He obviously wasn't the only one she'd impressed. But that didn't mean she was safe wandering around Scarborough unattended. This time, he didn't rein in when his horse began to canter.

He only wished that Scarborough's streets were straight and clear enough to make him comfortable with galloping. As it was, he had to weave his way around farmers bringing milk, eggs and produce to market. The wagons of fishmongers lumbered past, brine trailing like smoke in their wake, as they ferried Scarborough's catch inland. Still, he reached the harbor a short time later and guided his horse onto the firm sands.

The tide was low; he could not remember seeing it so far out. The stretch of gold seemed endless, the sails of the Scarborough fishing fleet mere dots on the horizon. Still, it was easy to spot the lone figure standing by the water's edge. What was she doing?

Clucking to his horse, he rode down the sands, leaping over debris from the storm and the occasional rock. As he approached, he could see that she was moving, but so slowly she scarcely took one step for four of his horse's. Her head was bowed, her hands clasped behind her back, and her skirts tucked up so that several inches of bare ankle and toes showed in the crisp morning air. He was so surprised he was reining in before her head snapped up.

"What are you doing?" she cried, rushing up the beach to him. Her hair was hastily tucked up on top of her head, gold strands flying every which way. He'd never realized gray eyes could look so fiery. "You get that great beast off this beach immediately!" She flung out an arm to point to the shore. "Immediately, sir!"

Her tone was so commanding, her face so determined, that Chase found himself complying without thinking. A shame Phoebe wasn't younger, he thought—Meredee Price would make an outstanding governess.

Or a captain at arms.

He rode his horse back to the road lining the shore, dismounted and tied the bay to the ornamental iron railing that stretched the length of the beach. She had returned to her slow dance with the waves. More curious than concerned, he hurried back to her side.

"Behind me," she ordered this time when he approached, and Chase fell obligingly, if mystified, in step behind her.

She took a step, head turning from side to side as if she were scanning the sands from about three feet to her left to the water's edge on her right. That must be why she wore no bonnet; it might obscure her vision. She had a strong profile, nose straight and firm, though dotted by freckles, chin a bit on the determined side. That came as no surprise. Though her simple blue dress was clean and neat, it was patched in places, as if it had been worn often and in difficult circumstances. Waves rolled up to tease her feet, brushing her bare skin like lover's fingers.

He snapped his gaze higher.

"What," he ventured, "are you searching for, Miss Price?"

"A *tellina incarnata,* my lord."

He struggled to remember his Latin. "And what would that be?"

"A seashell, Lord Allyndale."

Chase blinked. Then he increased his stride, grabbed her shoulder and spun her around. "Do you mean to tell me you ran away from my home, ordered me to abandon my horse and nearly scared the life out of me for a seashell!"

Meredee recoiled from him. His handsome face was florid, his blue eyes narrowed to slits. If he'd looked like that when she faced him across a dueling field, she thought she might have turned and fled, and honor be forfeited. She shook his hand off her shoulder, raised her head and took a step back. "I told Mrs. Downthistle when I left. You had no reason to be concerned."

"You leave before dawn and expect me not to wonder?"

"It was a good few minutes after dawn. And frankly, my lord, after your sister stomped back to her room with you last night, I thought you'd be relieved that I'd left."

"Nonsense." He seemed to be calming. The red was fading, and his breath came more slowly if the gentle rise and fall of his paisley waistcoat and bottle-green coat were any indication. "You were my guest. Of course I wished to know you were safe."

Meredee spread her hands. "As you can see, I'm fine. Thank you for your concern, and good day, my lord."

She turned, determined to put him out of her mind. She only had a short time. It wouldn't do to waste it mooning over the way the sun gilded his hair and the breeze ruffled it tenderly. Shading her eyes with one hand, she gazed down the shore toward the lighthouse instead. She still had a third of the bay to cover, and already the tide was a foot higher than when she'd started. Every day the tides grew closer together, more shallow. Every day her chances of finding the shell grew smaller.

Lord, help me!

"Are you really looking for seashells?" he asked with remarkable restraint behind her.

Meredee sighed. No one ever seemed to believe her quest. "Yes. A particular shell to be exact. The *tellina incarnata*, otherwise known as the carnation tellin." Just the name conjured up warmer waters and exotic shores. "It is a rare clam with a delicate pink shell." She scanned to the left and back to the right, then took another step as her father had taught her. She'd been so certain last night's storm would have washed a few ashore. Why couldn't she find one?

"And is there some reason you need this shell?"

Confusion laced every word. Meredee smiled to herself. Lord Allyndale clearly could not imagine anyone so devoted to shells. He'd never met her father.

"There is no need for you to tarry, my lord," she called back as she scanned and took another step. "I'm quite used to searching on my own."

"Does the shell hold some monetary value?"

This was beginning to feel like a game of twenty questions. She'd always been rather good at that game, but she wasn't entirely sure what she'd win if she stumped him now. "I believe some collectors would pay for the shell, but that's not my purpose in searching for it."

"Then does the shell have medicinal properties?"

My, but he was persistent. "None that I am aware of. Nor, before you ask, is it used for any industrial purpose. The *incarnata* only has value to me and a handful of conchologists around the Empire."

"Conchologists? Men of science who catalogue shells?"

Meredee took another step. "Not just men, my lord."

He was so quiet for a time that she thought perhaps he had abandoned her. She wouldn't have blamed him. Mrs. Price refused to brave the waves, and Algernon had long outgrown his amusement for the sport. She'd sometimes wondered why she'd bothered following her father on his hunts. He never acknowledged her presence, rarely responded to her questions with anything more than vague grunts. Oh, but when he found the perfect shell, when he knelt and drew it from the sands, his face held such an awed reverence that she knew she was looking at the very handiwork of God.

"Won't you tell me, Miss Price," he murmured, closer behind her than she'd thought, "why a seashell should require you to rise at dawn and roam the sands barefoot?"

Oh! She could feel her face heating in the cool morning air. Her feet had gone numb after the first quarter hour, and she'd completely forgotten the picture she must make. "I am barefoot," she managed with strained dignity, "the better to feel the sand and its treasures. Boots, like your horse's hooves, crush shells."

She risked a glance back and noticed that he was keeping his brown leather boots well away from the waves that slid in with the tide. They were not as stylish as she would have expected; worn, comfortable-looking, well-fitted to his large feet. She dared not look at his face to see what he thought of her explanation.

"I am impressed that you take this so seriously," he said, but she didn't hear another word. There! Just peeking from the moist sand, the thinnest edge of pink. Afraid even to breathe, she bent and brushed the grains of sand from the shell and lifted it into the sunlight.

The shell was long and thin and striped a vibrant shade of salmon pink, the edges pearlescent. It felt like fine porcelain against her trembling fingers. Then she looked closer, and her breath hissed out in a sigh. The right half was missing, cracked off in a jagged edge. Mcredee returned it to its place.

Lord Allyndale bent and retrieved it. "Ah, I see. It's broken. I suppose you need a whole shell."

Meredee nodded, afraid to talk lest she start crying. *Why can't I find one, Lord? Just one? I promised!*

Beside her, he glanced up and down the beach. A few people were venturing onto the sands, she saw, and the creak of wagon wheels heralded the arrival of the first bathing machines. Her time was running out.

"Still plenty of sand to go," he said as if to encourage her. "There must be more than one."

"Not necessarily," Meredee managed. She took a deep breath to steady herself. "My father searched for twenty years for this shell. It's common in the Mediterranean and along the African Coast, but it's been sighted in England only along the Yorkshire Coast. It was the one thing he regretted, dying when he did—that he'd never found the *incarnata*."

Lord Allyndale reached out and touched her chin, the leather of his gloves warm against her skin. He lifted her chin so that her gaze met his. His gaze was softer now, the blue deeper, like the depths of the North Sea but so much more alive. "I'm sure your father regretted more having to leave you."

Oh, how she wanted to believe that. Tears burned her eyes, and she had to look away, blinking them back. "I promised him I'd keep looking, that I'd find the *incarnata* for him. It was all he asked of me."

"Well, then," he said, hand falling away, "perhaps after we finish today we should try the North Bay tomorrow. I understand it is considerably less inhabited. Surely the shells there are more likely to remain undisturbed."

The North Bay! Oh, how she'd longed to try it, but Mrs. Price would never countenance such a use of their carriage, and Meredee was not much of a rider. She'd might as well have wished to visit the snows of Antarctica. Yet surely it would take much of the day to reach it and return. Would he really be so generous with his time, for no other reason than to further her quest?

She eyed him. His head was cocked, his gaze intent on hers. She'd never met a man other than her father who could so tightly focus his attention. She could imagine Chase Dearborn in Parliament, rallying his peers to his cause. Surely no one ever refused him anything.

"*We,* my lord?" she asked. "It might be messy. In fact, it might require you to muddy your boots."

"I never muddy my boots, Miss Price," he replied, but the twinkle in his eyes was unmistakable. "However, rest assured that I mean to accompany you. How could a gentleman in good conscience do otherwise? After all, if something threatened, you might have trouble running away barefooted."

She blushed at his teasing reminder of the state of her toes, dug into the golden sands. She should thank him for his kindness, ask him what time he'd like to leave, but something made her hesitate. If it were anyone else she knew offering her a trip to the North Bay, she would have jumped at the chance, barefoot or not. So why did she feel as if she should run away now, before this man came to mean too much to her? Before she began refining on what could only be a kindness?

She could feel him watching her, waiting for her answer. Oh, but she would not give in to these craven feelings, not when she had a chance to fulfill her promise to her father. She squared her shoulders and met Chase's gaze. "Very well, my lord. I would be delighted to accompany you to the North Bay."

She could only hope that she'd truly feel delight once she forced the butterflies from her stomach.

Chapter Seven

Both Algernon and Mrs. Price demanded an explanation of Meredee's disappearance when she returned to the inn later that morning. She found them in Mrs. Price's bedchamber, next to the sitting room they'd also engaged for their stay. Mrs. Price's room was the largest of the set, with creamy yellow walls and a dusky green-patterned carpet. With the deep green bed hangings on the walnut bed, Meredee often felt she'd wandered into a forest glade rather than a bedchamber.

Mrs. Price had retreated to the bed and sat against the carved headboard, pillows piled behind her, reading by the light of the south-facing window nearby. But when she heard Meredee's plans for the next day, she dropped her book and threw up her hands.

"Tell her, Algernon," she insisted, frowning at him where he stood gazing out the window. "Tell her that she cannot go jaunting about the countryside and ignore her duties."

Guilt's familiar fingers tugged at Meredee's heart. She glanced at her stepbrother to see if he also thought her trip was so ill-timed. He was dressed in his usual bright colors, his cravat tied in a complicated fold. But she did not like the pallor of his face.

"And what duties would those be, Mother?" Algernon inquired. He turned, spread his poppy-colored coattails, and took a seat on the curved-arm chair next to the bed. "Seeing to your least whim or compromising her principles to spy for me?"

Mrs. Price clutched her lacy robe near her heart, as if he'd sorely wounded her. Meredee reached out from where she sat on her stepmother's bed and touched the knee of his cinnamon-colored trousers. "Is something wrong, Algernon?"

He shrugged. "Just a little bluedeviled." He nodded toward the bed. "Forgive me, Mother. I'm locked in a box with the world passing me by. It's making me churlish."

"Well, certainly," Mrs. Price said, lowering her hand. "But you mustn't fret, dearest. Lord Allyndale shows no inclination to repeat his threats. I believe you may be safe in showing your face."

Meredee nodded, withdrawing her touch. "Perhaps if you spoke to him, Algernon."

Her stepbrother rose and began his pacing, the shine of his high-topped boots flashing with each step. "Not yet. He was here this morning, looking for someone. I don't think he saw me, but he rode out of here fast. If only I could be sure I wasn't the source of his urgency."

Mrs. Price heaved a sigh. "Then I suppose Meredee must go with him tomorrow. And I shall have to go along as chaperone."

Algernon paused. "What about Allyndale's sister?"

"I'm not sure Lady Phoebe would appreciate traveling to the North Bay," Meredee said, trying to envision the girl standing still long enough to spy the *incarnata*.

"Nonsense," Algernon said, resuming his pacing. "I have it on good authority that she is a bruising rider. I'm sure she'd be delighted to accompany you."

Meredee had a hard time imagining Phoebe as a bruising anything, but Algernon seemed to have made up his mind, for he rubbed his hands together with obvious glee. "Yes, this will serve all our purposes nicely. You have a chaperone, and Mother can avoid exposure to the elements."

He was entirely too delighted with himself. "And what do you gain?" Meredee asked.

His smile blossomed. "Why the knowledge that the Dearborns are safely occupied. Freedom, dear sister. Freedom!"

To Meredee's surprise, Lady Phoebe was delighted to accompany them the next day. Her response to

Meredee's note was filled with exclamation points and capital letters. "We shall have the BEST Time!!!" Meredee began to hope she was right.

Lord Allyndale himself drove into the coaching yard a little before seven that morning. Given the route they must travel to reach the bay, they had to leave early to catch even a portion of the morning's low tide. His jaunty curricle was painted a deep yellow with gilt appointments and seats of brown tooled leather. A regal groom rode behind, and the two perfectly matched black horses at the front looked ready to run. Unlike Algernon, the earl was dressed in a sensible gray tweed wool coat and chamois breeches buttoned at the knee. His smile as Meredee came out of the inn to greet him told her he was just as eager for their adventure.

It seemed that Algernon was right about Lady Phoebe's love of riding, for she was dressed in a habit of fine blue wool trimmed with black braid and seated on a dainty roan mare. She adjusted her plumed riding hat to a rakish angle on her curls and beamed at Meredee. "To find the elusive *incarnata!*"

Meredee was ready. She'd worn the practical blue cotton gown she used when hunting, a straw bonnet to shield her from the sun along the way and her high boots. She also carried her supplies in her father's brown leather case. The groom hopped down to help her store it in the boot, and Lord Allyndale watched from his seat.

"I thought perhaps we'd need provisions as well," he said when she eyed the wicker hamper taking up half the space.

"And do you intend to stay a fortnight?" she teased.

He smiled as he climbed down to help Meredee into the carriage. "As long as it takes to see you triumphant, Miss Price."

He handed her up onto the seat and took his place beside her. She'd only ridden in an open carriage a few times, and never with such a handsome gentleman beside her. She found herself acutely aware of his body near hers, the least movement of his hands as he took up the reins and released the brake. When he flashed her a grin, her answering smile felt wobbly.

Phoebe was turning her horse to take up position as if she were their outrider. "I told him we could bring the coachman and the traveling coach," she confided to Meredee, leaning precariously out of her seat as she passed. "But he insisted it was more fun to drive himself."

"And how else am I to prove to Miss Price that I'm not some vain popinjay more interested in my clothes than my company?" he responded with a raised brow and a twinkle in his eyes.

Was that why he objected to Algernon? Hardly enough reason to threaten a duel! And who was he to talk? Algernon might parade about in fancy clothes, but that didn't stop him from doing what was necessary. Lord Allyndale refused to muddy his boots!

But he was a crack driver. He threaded the curricle through the busy streets so smoothly she found she could relax against the seat and merely enjoy the ride. The sun was slanting through morning clouds, warming the air and gilding this building and that in shafts of light. Meredee clasped her gloved hands in her lap and sighed with pure pleasure.

"You said you'd spent some time in Scarborough," he ventured as they started up the hill out of town. "I must admit this is my first visit."

"I feel as if it's nearly my first visit," Meredee replied. "So much has changed in the last five years, the lamps to light the streets at night, the new public gardens. But some things remain the same." She pointed to the square stone tower rising to the right of the carriage. "That's St. Mary's."

"And what is special about St. Mary's?"

"My parents were married there for one," she offered. "And they have a choir of orphans who sing on Sundays."

"Then I must take care to have us back in time for services tomorrow."

Meredee smiled at the teasing tone. "You must take care to have us back by supper, my lord. My stepmother will have apoplexy otherwise."

He chuckled. "And Mrs. Price did not wish to join us today?"

"No, indeed. Nor would she wish to visit the wilds of Africa, which I am persuaded she equates with the North Bay. But I can hardly wait."

The blacks seemed to sense her eagerness, for they pulled the curricle swiftly up the hill and out into open country. The gentle fields were covered in short grass where creamy sheep wandered. Lady Phoebe called the occasional question as they rode along. She perched on her little mare as easily as on a padded chair in her drawing room. Meredee still had trouble imagining the girl taking fences and pounding over rough terrain, but she certainly seemed comfortable on the sidesaddle.

They reached the North Bay by nine, having stopped once in a copse of trees to rest the horses. The road roughened as they approached, winding down through overhanging trees to break out onto the shore and sunlight. As at the South Bay, the hillside edging the North Bay curved in a crescent that dipped in the middle and rose in higher and higher cliffs on either side, ending at the castle headland on the south and a rocky outcropping on the north. With the tide out, the arc of sand seemed to stretch for miles, the expanse broken by uneven lumps of dark rock and pockets of tidal pools. The only sound was the whisper of the waves. Not a soul was in sight. Meredee pressed her fingers to her lips in wonder.

As soon as the carriage rolled to a stop along the cliff side, she began preparing herself for the search.

While the groom settled the horses, she retrieved her father's case, pulled out pins to hoist up her skirts and removed her bonnet.

"Not barefoot this time?" Lord Allyndale asked when she came around from behind the curricle.

"Not today. The sands on the South Bay are some of the firmest around. I don't know what I'll find here."

He glanced down at his boots with a frown.

Meredee smiled. "If you stay away from the tide's edge, my lord, you should be able to save them."

He shook his head. "I see my driving failed to impress. What a vain creature you must think me. It's just that I find it difficult to locate boots that actually fit comfortably. This pair was made by a master bootmaker who has since passed on, and his apprentice is not in his master's league."

"Ah, so you are being practical. Then let me give you another practical task. We would be wise to find two tree limbs down from the storm—about six feet long and fairly straight."

"You go right ahead," Lady Phoebe said, patting her horse where she stood beside it. "I will freely admit to any amount of vanity so long as I do not have to ruin my riding habit." With a giggle, she walked up the beach into the shade of some trees and sat on a grassy tuffet where the groom had spread a blanket.

The last thing Meredee did was take out a bottle of

ointment and rub it over her exposed neck, face and hands. The earl took a sniff and recoiled.

"Tell me this somehow attracts mollusks," he said, arm half raised as if to cover his nose.

Meredee laughed. "On the contrary—it repels, my lord."

"I'd never have guessed." Something must have buzzed nearby, for he slapped at his ear.

Meredee held out the bottle. "Here, you may need this. All this brackish water attracts any manner of insects. My father swore this ointment kept them away."

"I can believe it." He shook his head. "But I should be fine without it. Gnats are no strangers to the moors."

"Is that where your estate lies?" Meredee asked as they set off down the shore. The breeze brushed her cheeks, bringing with it the tang of brine.

"On the north moors, yes. Just outside Great Ayton. Like looking across the sea here, the sky seems to go on forever, and it's so quiet you can hear the birds calling."

She could not miss the ache in his voice. "How kind you are to escort your sister about society instead."

He was quiet a moment, taking her hand to help her over a ridge of rock that rose a foot out of the sand. When they reached the other side, he did not release her, pulling her up short. "You are the kind one, Miss Price. You befriend Phoebe, you keep your stepmother company, you allow me to take part in your dreams. I have never met anyone like you."

The timbre of his voice, so full of wonder, touched a place inside her she'd all but forgotten. "You honor me, my lord."

He peered down into her eyes. "Are we perhaps beyond *my lord* and *Miss Price?* My friends use my given name, Chase. May I count you as one of them?"

It was a courtesy, but suddenly she felt as if she'd been peering through windows for years, watching life go on for other people. He offered to let her in, to let her close. Did she dare open herself to him, take a chance that this time might be different? Worse, her stepbrother's fears lay like a shadow over her. Would Chase Dearborn want to be her friend, want to be anywhere near her if her knew who she was?

His blue eyes clouded, and he released her hand. "Forgive me. I have obviously overstepped my bounds."

"No, no," Meredee hurried to assure him. "I am delighted you consider me a friend, my…Chase. You must call me Meredee."

A smile grew, more breathtaking than the sweep of the sea. "It would be a pleasure."

A wave splashed Meredee's boot, and Chase dodged out of its way. "Well," she said with a laugh.

"I take that to mean we should get back to work. Let's see what we can find, shall we?"

For the next two hours, they roamed the sands side by side. She showed him the feathery tongue of feeding barnacles, the dark shine of mussels clustering on rocky outcroppings, and the scuttling walk of clever hermit crabs who also liked to appropriate shells. With each wonder, his smile grew wider, his gaze more intense. He was the one who pointed out silver fingerlings darting in the shallows, the spout out at sea that might have been a passing whale. With her father, she'd been an observer, someone to marvel at his finds. With Chase, she was a participant, a partner. She'd never felt so alive.

At length, he looked toward the trees with a frown. "Where's Phoebe gotten to?"

He sounded more annoyed than concerned, but Meredee straightened from where she'd been examining a tidal pool and scanned the shore, as well. "Perhaps waiting bored her. We have been at it a while."

His frown deepened. "Would you mind returning to the carriage for a moment? She's probably asleep on the cushions, but I'd like to make certain."

Knowing how much he worried about his sister, Meredee nodded. "Some food and drink would be most welcome. And perhaps we can persuade Lady Phoebe to join us."

He grinned at her. "You'd have better luck getting me to slather on your dire concoction."

"Ah, but I'm not the one who'll need salve tonight," she countered, pointing to a series of raised welts along his collar.

He put his hand to his neck and grimaced. "Fustian! Ah, well. A small price to pay for a glorious morning."

But when they'd made their way back to the carriage, Lady Phoebe and her horse were nowhere in sight. His groom, who had been walking the carriage horses along the shore, was surprised to find her gone, as well.

"Confound the girl!" Chase climbed onto the carriage step and craned his neck to look in all directions. "Phoebe! Phoebe Dearborn, answer me!"

Gulls rocketed up from the sands, but nothing else moved along the shore. Where was Lady Phoebe?

"She can't have gone far," Meredee reasoned. "Perhaps if you go north and I go south, we'll find her faster."

"Excellent plan. Perkins, stay here in case she returns." Chase jumped down from the carriage and strode off up the beach, his shouts echoing back to her.

Did he have cause for such concern? They'd seen no one all morning except a few fishermen heading out to sea. Was it truly more dangerous here than she'd thought? Then why agree to let her set off alone?

Keeping her stick close, she headed to the south, calling the girl's name. She heard no answer, but soon she saw the clear indentation of a horseshoe in the sand at the edge of the bush where the cliff broke in a wooded ravine. Why had Lady Phoebe gone that way? Had something piqued her curiosity?

Glancing back, Meredee found that she could no longer see Perkins or Chase. Perhaps she should simply find Lady Phoebe and return as soon as possible.

The bush was broken and trampled as if a horse had recently come through it. She easily followed the trail along a little creek that bubbled down the bed of the ravine. Trees crowded on either side, cutting off the sun and wrapping Meredee in twilight. She was glad when, a moment later, the path opened into a small clearing. As Meredee ducked under tree limbs into the space, Lady Phoebe wheeled her horse to face her.

"Oh, Meredee," she cried, eyes wide. "You gave me such a fright!"

"And you gave your brother a fright by disappearing like this," Meredee countered, straightening.

"I'm sorry, but it was the only way." She beamed at Meredee. "You see, he does return my affections!"

For a moment, Meredee could only stare at her, confused, then the girl's meaning burst upon her. Phoebe wasn't alone. She hadn't come to the clearing out of curiosity. She'd come to meet a man.

The man Chase Dearborn had dragged his sister to Scarborough to escape was here, now. Meredee took a step away and felt the bush at her back. The fellow had to be watching her. Her muscles tensed, demanding that she run, escape.

She put out a hand. "Come with me, Phoebe. Please. There must be a better way."

"But you needn't be afraid," Phoebe assured her. "He'd never hurt you of all people."

The bushes rustled behind the girl, and Meredee clutched her staff. A tall fellow with an impossibly red coat and purple trousers stepped into the clearing, his cravat tied in a complicated fold.

"Hello, sister," Algernon said.

Chapter Eight

"Algernon!" Meredee cried, taking a step toward him. "What have you done!"

"Nothing terrible!" Lady Phoebe protested before Meredee's stepbrother could respond. "He followed me here. Don't you see? He loves me!"

Algernon had the good sense to look abashed. "I fear it's bellows to mend. One look at my lass, and I was lost."

Meredee wanted to grab her stepbrother by the arm and drag him fully into the light. "Then why run away to Scarborough? Why not speak to Lord Allyndale, and tell him your intentions are honorable?"

"I did!"

"And?" Meredee challenged.

Algernon hung his head. "And that's when he told me if he ever saw my face again, I could expect a call from his seconds."

"You see what a bully my brother has become, Meredee?" Lady Phoebe cried.

Meredee wasn't sure what she saw. Was this why Chase kept his sister so close? Did he expect Algernon to follow her, to sneak behind his back in this detestable manner? What did that say for her stepbrother?

"I still believe your brother has your best interests at heart, Lady Phoebe," she insisted. "Can you say the same, Algernon?"

Her stepbrother clapped a hand to the chest of his crimson jacket. Even in subterfuge he remained true to his fashion sense. It was a wonder they hadn't spotted him following them!

"Me?" he protested. "I have the very best of intentions, I promise you! I'd like nothing better than to marry the girl!"

Lady Phoebe squealed, then had to spend a moment getting her horse back under control, as Algernon clucked in obvious admiration.

Dear Lord, neither of them has the sense of a cricket! Give me the words to dissuade them.

In the distance, Meredee heard Chase's voice. He still called his sister's name, but now it alternated with hers.

"We must go," she said. "Algernon, return to the inn. I cannot imagine that Lord Allyndale would want to discuss anything with you now. Lady Phoebe, come with me."

"You will ask me to marry you again properly, won't you, Algernon?" the girl begged as he started back to where his horse was evidently waiting.

"I'd like to see anyone stop me," he proclaimed, then winced as Chase yelled, close at hand. "Think of me often?"

"Every moment," Lady Phoebe pledged, eyes shining with fervor.

"Go!" Meredee ordered, pointing to the bush. Algernon scrambled out of the clearing.

Lady Phoebe heaved a maidenly sigh but showed no interest in budging beyond the spot where she could watch Algernon's retreating back. Meredee snatched the reins from her hands and pulled the horse forward. "This way. Now."

"You begin to sound like my brother," Lady Phoebe complained, but she suffered herself to be led to the beach.

Chase met them at the edge of the ravine. Sweat shone along his face, dampening his hair to brown. "What's happened?" he demanded, taking Lady Phoebe's reins from Meredee. "Phoebe, are you all right?"

His sister waved a hand. "I'm fine. I was merely looking for some fresh water for my horse. It is terribly hot out here."

"You should have told us or Perkins," Chase replied, and Meredee could see a muscle working in his jaw as if he were clamping his teeth between comments. "It isn't safe for you to wander off."

Lady Phoebe sighed and sagged in her seat. "Oh, I know. I shudder to think what would have happened if Meredee hadn't come upon me. I might never have found my way back to the carriage."

Chase paled at that, but Meredee shook her head. "Nonsense. You'd merely have turned your horse and followed your own trail back to the beach."

Lady Phoebe perked up. "Oh, of course! How silly of me. Why didn't I think of that?"

"Why indeed?" Chase muttered between clenched teeth. He handed the reins back to her and pointed to the north. "There's a deeper stream of water coming from the cliffs along there. I suggest you see to your horse and then return to the coach. That is, if you think you can find it."

Meredee cringed at the sarcastic tone, but his sister peered down the shore. "Oh, yes. I should be able to see you from there. Back in a bit." She clucked to her horse and started down the sand.

What was wrong with the girl? Meredee could not believe she was so scatterbrained. Was it all a performance for Chase? But why? Surely Lady Phoebe knew that the more helpless she seemed, the more her brother worked at protecting her.

"We should start back," he said with a frown toward the trees. Meredee glanced that way as well, afraid she'd see a telltale red coat among the green.

But Algernon had apparently decamped, for all she saw were the trees waving in the breeze.

"I believe you're right, my lord," she said, then turned to follow him back toward the coach. It was not until they'd reached the carriage that she realized he hadn't protested the use of his title over his name.

She put away her things as Perkins watered the carriage horses and Chase collected his sister. Then they set off back up the draw to the main road.

"I regret we couldn't find your shell," Chase said to Meredee as the carriage bumped over the rough road. "Thank you for understanding about Phoebe."

But she didn't understand—not completely. She could certainly see that if his sister refused to show any good sense, he had little choice but to try to save her from herself. The burden was obvious, even for him, yet Phoebe made no move to correct his impression and ease his concerns. Even now she seemed oblivious to the fact that she had distressed him.

"Why must we hurry?" Phoebe complained from her saddle as they rolled along the main road. "It's a lovely day, and everything is so delightful! There's not another soul for miles! We could be the only people in the Empire."

"Nonsense," Chase called back. "There's a fellow on the road ahead of us. I've spotted his red coat twice on a straightaway."

Meredee glanced over to Lady Phoebe and saw

the same alarm on her face. The girl shook herself and reined in. "Well, I'm not going another step," she called after the retreating carriage. "You promised me a picnic!"

Chase pulled his horses to a stop. He sat perfectly still for a moment as if putting a similar rein on his temper, then turned to meet Meredee's concerned gaze. "Do you mind?"

He looked so tight and overdrawn she would have done anything to return him to the eager fellow who had hunted shells with her that morning. "Not at all," she assured him. "A picnic would be delightful, and it would be a shame to waste the food you brought. An old friend of the family, Mr. Openshaw, owns a field up ahead on the right. I'm sure he won't mind if we use it."

"Perfect!" Lady Phoebe said, sunny mood miraculously restored. "I'll meet you there." With a cry, she urged her horse into a gallop and shot past them.

Chase's face was grim as he turned toward the front of the carriage again. "I must apologize for my sister," he said as they started off. "She frequently acts without thinking."

"The trait can be endearing," Meredee offered.

"Or annoying." He cast her a quick glance. "Forgive me for forcing you from the shore, Meredee. You are the one bright spot in this day."

Her heart lightened inside her. The feeling only

strengthened as he brought the carriage to a gentle stop beside the grassy field.

They were high enough above Scarborough that she could see over the fields and out into the North Sea. Clouds floated on the horizon, their puffs like the billowing sails of ships plying the waters of the bay. Somewhere in the distance a cow lowed, and closer at hand swallows dipped and chirped. Lady Phoebe wandered the grass, plucking daisies.

"I fear I have no fine table at which to seat you, my lady," Chase said, as Perkins set down the hamper at Meredee's feet. Chase pulled a blue wool blanket from the top, shook it out and spread it on the grass.

"At least you're not asking me to eat off your cloak, gallant sir," she replied, kneeling beside him.

The hamper was compartmented so that one end was lined with metal and filled with ice to keep the rest cool. There was broccoli salad with pickled nasturtium buds and bright flowers nestled among the greens, cold chicken rubbed with herbs, loaves of crisp-crusted bread, gingerbread cakes and tart lemonade.

"How lovely!" Lady Phoebe cried as she joined them. She toppled her daisies into Meredee's lap and collapsed onto the blanket. Chase snatched up the bottle of lemonade before it fell and shook his head at his sister in pure exasperation.

Conversation flowed easily, warm as the sunlight that blessed the meadow. Chase leaned back on his elbows and gazed off into the distance, one hand toying with the stem of one of Phoebe's daisies. The breeze caressed his hair, sweeping a lock away from his face.

"The world is far bigger than we believe," he murmured. "The amount of life in those tiny tidal pools you showed me today amazes me. What more could we see if we but looked?"

This was the man she was coming to respect, to admire. "I've often thought that it's true that all creation sings His praise," Meredee replied. "We just need to listen."

Lady Phoebe stretched like a cat. "Well, I am quite ready to listen. In fact, I'm so contented I'm certain I haven't the strength to ride back."

Chase chuckled, straightening and tossing down the flower. "A shame, my girl, but you would bring your horse."

Phoebe shrugged. "I could just tie Belle to the coach and climb inside."

Chase eyed her. "And where do you suggest Miss Price sit?"

"Up on the bench, with me, of course," she said with an airy wave of her hand. "And that means you can ride Belle back." She turned to Meredee, oblivious to the frown growing on her brother's face. "You don't mind, do you, dear Meredee? I'm certain you must be tired of my brother's company by now."

"Phoebe," Chase started warningly.

Meredee glanced between them. "I'm delighted to keep either of you company while you drive. But I'm certain I'll never tire of your brother's company."

As soon as she said it, she realized that she sounded far too forward and dropped her gaze. He'd think she was as giddy as Phoebe!

"I assure you, Meredee," he murmured, "I feel the same way."

She dared to glance up at him. A smile was once again playing on his lips, and a light brightened the blue of his eyes.

"Oh," Lady Phoebe said knowingly, delicate brows arched. "Well, I know when I'm *de trop.* I suppose I'll have to ride back after all."

"Yes," Chase said, gaze on Meredee's. "You will."

Meredee found it difficult to focus on packing up the leftovers. Her hands kept clasping together as if to hold tight to the feelings tumbling through her. She had to get over this unreasonable fear! Just because the one man she'd chosen to love as a girl had left her didn't mean that Chase would do the same. If God was kind enough to give her another chance at love, she should take it. She placed the last plate into the hamper and shut the lid on it and on her feelings.

Chase didn't seem to notice her agitation. While Perkins stowed the hamper, Chase helped his sister into the sidesaddle, then came around to help Meredee into the curricle. This time the touch at her waist as he lifted her set her pulse to pounding, and her hands trembled as she arranged her skirts.

As Chase reached for the reins, Lady Phoebe took up position as their outrider again. Her head was high, her focus on the horizon. Sunlight glowed in her complexion, highlighted her lashes.

"She looks like an angel leading the heavenly forces into battle," Meredee said as Chase clucked to the horses and they started back.

"You still say that after what you've seen today?" Chase asked. "Sometimes I despair of her."

"Surely she has more sense than you give her credit for," she suggested.

"If she has, I've yet to be shown evidence of it."

"She's young," Meredee offered. "Not even twenty, I imagine."

"She's all of nineteen. But age is no excuse. Were you this giddy at that age?"

She'd almost have liked to have been. But at nineteen, she'd ready known heartache, from losing the man she thought she might love. "I didn't have the luxury of being giddy," she told him. "My father had taken ill by then, and I was busy nursing him. Picnics and parties seem far away from a sickroom."

He gave his attention to the horses for a moment, guiding them down the hill toward the edges of Scarborough. "Your stepmother could not care for him?"

There was more concern than censure in the question. "Oh, she was right beside me. She urged me to rest, but I didn't wish to leave him. It was clear that he wouldn't be with us much longer. Every moment was precious."

"My father died when I was twelve," he said, gaze out over his horses' heads. "Hunting accident. I was away at school at the time. I never had the opportunity to say goodbye, to ask his advice. I envy you that."

Twelve. Then he'd been the head of the family for many years. Lady Phoebe could have been no more than one or two. Neither of the Dearborns had mentioned a mother alive and waiting for them, so it seemed the only family Lady Phoebe had known was Chase. Small wonder he felt responsible for her.

"That must have been a burden, taking on responsibilities so young," she told him.

He quirked a smile. "I was born to those responsibilities. If they became mine sooner than expected, it was only a question of timing, never of duty."

"You wear them well."

His smile broadened. "In truth, I enjoy them. Ensuring that the estate flourishes, keeping government working during these trying times, those are challenges a man can relish."

She could see him standing before Parliament, hand upraised, arguing for a better way. "And yet here you are, in Scarborough."

He gave the horses their heads as if to speed them toward a greater goal. "Only for a time. I have every

hope of leaving before summer's end and returning
to my duties. But what of you? The day you saved
Phoebe, you mentioned you didn't know when you'd
leave Scarborough. How long will your stepmother be
willing to bathe in the sea and drink the waters?"

Meredee laughed. "I have never heard anyone talk
about the Scarborough waters with exactly that tone.
Do you find them so noxious?"

"Let us merely say, my dear Meredee, that I suspect
the same person who concocted your father's insect
elixir developed the recipe for the spa waters."

"You are doing it entirely too brown. Those waters
have healing properties. Look at Mr. Barriston."

"A more wrinkled specimen I have yet to find."

Meredee shook her finger at him. "And may you
look so good when you reach the age of eighty and
eight, sir."

He laughed. "All right, I'll grant you that Mr. Barriston is remarkable for his longevity."

"And Mr. Dickinson, who was governor of the
spa years ago, attained the age of one hundred and
one."

He shook his head. "You clearly know the history
of the spa. And can you promise me that it will heal
everyone who drinks of it?"

Her father's face came to mind, and she felt her
smile slipping. "I wish I could."

He reached out his free hand and covered hers with
it. "Forgive me. I should make better conversation."

His touch focused her. How could she mourn the past when the present was so very sweet? "I find the conversation and the company quite satisfactory," she replied.

He gave her hands a squeeze and released her, but she fancied she could still feel his grip, firm, gentle, encouraging. She held the sensation to her heart.

They dipped into Scarborough, and she could see the red-tiled roofs sloping down the hill, the golden stone tower of St. Mary's and the outline of the castle on the headland.

Up ahead, the lone figure in the red coat was all too visible as he slipped deeper into town. Meredee's heart jumped. The rest of the conversation, she feared, was far more stilted, and she could not relax until Chase had deposited her at the inn and driven for home.

Chapter Nine

"Tell me something," Chase said to Phoebe as soon as they'd returned to the house and he'd had Beagan and the footmen deal with their accoutrements. "Why did you join us today?"

His sister, about to climb the stairs for her room, paused to look back at him wide-eyed. "Why, I wanted to see the North Bay, of course."

Chase raised his brows. "Indeed. That would explain why you spent much of the time wandering into ravines and less in befriending Miss Price."

Phoebe smiled. "She is a dear, isn't she? I do hope you plan to offer for her soon."

Chase shook his head. "Any plans I have for matrimony will have to wait until you are settled in that happy state."

Phoebe's smile only grew bigger, and she hurried back to his side where he stood in the marble-tiled entryway. "Oh, Chase, really? Then you've had second thoughts about Algernon?"

Chase rubbed the bridge of his nose. "Mr. Whitaker is not a topic of discussion in this house."

"Oh!" Phoebe stamped her foot. "You are the most unreasonable, pigheaded man! I hope you enjoy eating dinner alone, for I shall *not* be joining you." She dashed up the stairs, and Chase heard her door slam a few moments later.

"Why can't my sister be more reasonable?" he grumbled to Trevor when his friend joined him for dinner in the cherub-ceilinged dining room. "Would you wish to marry a dandy like Whitaker?"

"Never," Trevor returned, the sleeve of his navy coat dark against the table linens as he reached for another helping of veal. "The person I marry had better not need to shave in the mornings."

"I wasn't aware that Whitaker was old enough to shave."

"A direct hit!" Trevor declared. "But just because you and I find Whitaker tiresome doesn't mean Lady Phoebe will follow suit. Women have their own opinions in these matters."

"So I've noticed. I suppose I should just be glad Whitaker is less dangerous than Delacorte. I doubt he'd have the stomach to kidnap her." Chase tugged the edge of his linen shirt away from the insect bites that dotted his neck. They itched abominably, and he'd finally settled on his tobacco-colored banyan to wear to dinner. The embroidered long coat was comfortable, and it allowed him to forgo a cravat.

"Your sister does seem to attract scoundrels," Trevor agreed with an utter lack of concern over the matter. "You're lucky she's never shown interest in me."

Chase eyed him. "Perhaps I should encourage her then."

Trevor sat up so suddenly he nearly pulled his china plate into his lap. "That was a joke."

"Not necessarily." Chase leaned forward. "I've always maintained that a marriage should be for mutual benefit, the couple well known to each other. You've known Phoebe since she was a baby; she listens to your guidance. You could help her mature."

Trevor's eyes narrowed. "And how exactly do I benefit, besides having married an adorable infant?"

Chase leaned back. "She has a considerable dowry, and our family is irreproachable."

Trevor set down his glass, folded his napkin and rose. "If that's all you think I wish in a wife, Lord Allyndale, I bid you good evening."

Chase rose and caught him before he could stalk out the door. "Hang on! I meant no insult."

"You seldom do." Trevor's green eyes snapped fire. "But you are one of the few who knows the nature of my birth and the state of my finances, and I'll thank you not to mention either again."

Chase let go of his arm. "You know neither

troubles me. You've proven yourself an honorable gentleman."

"Then believe me when I say I can handle my own affairs."

"And believe me when I say I only wish to help."

Trev shook his head. "I'd be mad to accept your help. I've watched you since we were boys. When a problem arises, you set it right, no matter the cost to you or those around you. You cannot order the world to your convenience, Allyndale. The rest of us have opinions and desires, as well."

Chase stepped back. "You sound like Phoebe."

"Then perhaps your sister has more sense than you think."

Chase sighed. "Come back to the table, Trev. All I ask is that you think on the matter. By marrying Phoebe, I am convinced, you'd be doing my sister and yourself a great service. I know you could protect her against the likes of Delacorte."

"You and I together can handle Delacorte," Trevor replied, but he suffered himself to return to the table. "As for the rest, I still say you should hire Miss Price to chaperone your sister. Surely someone so redoubtable could keep away the riffraff like Whitaker."

"Miss Price has her own plans for the summer," Chase told him. "She seeks a particular seashell."

Trevor choked and had to reach for his glass. "Oh, I can see how that would make it difficult to spend time in society," he said sarcastically after taking a good long sip. "You'd be doing her a favor by pairing her with your sister. Talk about mutual benefit!"

Chase wasn't sure how Meredee would be helped by pairing her with Phoebe, but the idea took root. He resolved to discuss it with Meredee at the next opportunity.

Meredee was having similar trouble getting her point across. She fully intended to discuss Algernon's behavior with him the moment she returned to the inn, but when she carried her things back to her room, she found his room empty. She would have been worried, but the red jacket folded carefully across the chair told her that her stepbrother had come back safely, if only to change his coat.

"He is woefully neglectful of his duty," Mrs. Price lamented when Meredee asked her stepmother if she'd seen Algernon. She sniffed and eyed Meredee from where she'd taken to her bed with a headache. "I wonder where he learned that."

Meredee felt the barb, as she was certain her stepmother intended. "I am sorry to have spent so much time away from you today. But were you not to go walking with Mr. Cranell?"

Her stepmother pouted, reminding Meredee a bit of Lady Phoebe. "His gout flared up. And Colonel Williams was busy with his tailor."

Meredee stuck out her lower lip in sympathy.

"And so Scarborough's reigning belle found herself unexpectedly alone."

Her stepmother nodded. "Exactly! You may read to me if you like, or perhaps we could work on the lace for my new cap."

"Are you not the least bit curious about my adventure today?" Meredee teased.

Mrs. Price blinked. "No. Why? Did his lordship say something about me? Or Algernon?"

"No," Meredee replied, holding back her sigh. "But I need to speak to Algernon as soon as he returns."

"I'm sure I don't know why. *He* didn't tarry at the inn alone all day. He took himself off before I woke and only returned long enough to tell me not to wait up."

And in this, at least, Algernon proved true to his word. Though Meredee stayed up until her candle burned out, her stepbrother didn't return to the inn until after she'd fallen asleep.

She was ready to wake him for services the next morning, but Mrs. Price intervened.

"Don't you bother him," her stepmother said, her gray lustring gown nearly as severe as her words. She settled her white straw bonnet on her curls. "He's so worried about this affair with Lord Allyndale he cannot get enough rest."

Somehow Meredee did not think it was worry that kept her stepbrother abed. But she picked up her cashmere shawl with the pink roses along the hem, draped it over her pale rose gown, and followed her stepmother down to the cart the inn used to ferry its guests around town.

St. Mary's at least was unchanged from when Meredee had last lived in Scarborough. The dark wood pews with their little gated entries sat under triple arches of golden stone, bathed in light from the massive stained-glass windows that edged the sanctuary. The voices of the orphan choir rose sweetly toward the high-beamed ceiling. It was a place to inspire awe, instill reverence. She always came away feeling as if she were better than when she'd arrived.

Glancing about now, she spotted Mr. Cranell, whose pallor and grimace said his leg still pained him; Colonel Williams looked dapper in a new bottle-green coat; and Mrs. Warden and Mrs. Dennings, the widows who made their living by pouring the waters for the spa guests, were on hand, as well. Mrs. Dennings, in particular, looked weary, her shoulders bowed, her head sunken onto her chest. She was a sharp contrast to William Barriston, who stood tall and strong in his pew near the front of the church alongside his narrow wife.

No sooner had Meredee sighted the Barristons than she noticed another tall, well-shaped gentleman nearby. Chase wore his black coat with dignity, his head high, his profile a study in concentration. Lady

Phoebe beside him yawned behind her lace-gloved hand, head bowed under her pink satin bonnet.

Though Meredee listened with her usual care to the readings and the vicar's sermon, her gaze kept drifting toward Chase. She saw when he handed his sister the book of prayer, the movement encouraging. She noticed when he bowed his head for the benediction. Far from detracting from the service, his presence added to the simple pleasure of worship by knowing that he was worshipping, too.

A deep sigh of satisfaction rose up inside her as she followed her stepmother out of the church. St. Mary's sat near the castle headland and commanded a view out over the town to the sea. The sky was a brilliant blue over Scarborough; the water a deeper blue stretching out below them. For a moment, she wished she were a bird, soaring up and over the expanse, with limitless light and limitless freedom. Then she noticed the man in the yellow coat, darting behind one of the nearby tombstones in the churchyard, and all good feelings fled.

Algernon.

What was he doing? He couldn't be bothered to attend services, to pay his respects to his Maker, yet here he was, skulking about the churchyard like a resurrection man set on stealing corpses. She glanced at Mrs. Price, but she did not seem to have noticed her son, as she was still talking about how much she enjoyed the Vicar Mr. Kirk's way with words.

"Wasn't that lovely?" Lady Phoebe enthused, hurrying up to them. "Those dear children, and the organ! A shame so many people were missing."

Her gaze to Meredee was imploring, and Meredee realized with a start that she was worried that Algernon hadn't attended.

"I fear the attractions of Scarborough keep many abed late," Meredee said, and nearly winced when her voice came out more stern than she intended.

Lady Phoebe frowned, but Chase joined them then. His smile was all for Meredee, and she found it difficult to remember Algernon's problems.

"I'm merely thankful our exertions yesterday did not keep you from attending, Miss Price," he said. "I wonder—you've known the town some years. I find myself curious as to the families buried here. Would you be so good as to show me?"

He truly wanted a guided tour of the churchyard? Not now, not with Algernon hiding there. Lady Phoebe glanced in that direction, and her hand shot out and gripped Meredee's arm. "Oh, yes," she said, gaze focused on the tombstones. "I love old churchyards."

Chase frowned so thoroughly at his sister that she nodded vigorously. "Truly! I'm sure Meredee knows any number of stories. Don't you?"

At the moment, she was privy to one story too many. "Much as I adore St. Mary's," Meredee said,

"I'm sure the churchyard would hold little interest for either of you."

Mrs. Price suddenly clutched her other arm. "No, no. Of course not." She jerked her head theatrically toward the tombstones, and Meredee nearly closed her eyes in mortification. "I'm sure we would be much better served to stay here and chat."

"Nonsense," Lady Phoebe said with determined cheerfulness. "This way." She tugged Meredee toward the graves.

"I must insist," Mrs. Price said, clinging on to her other hand. Meredee held herself still, arms tense, refusing to be budged by either of them.

"If you'll allow me," Chase said. He reached out and detached his sister's then Mrs. Price's determined grips. "Miss Price will accompany me. Phoebe, you will wait by the carriage. Mrs. Price, I promise to restore your stepdaughter to you shortly."

"Well, if you think you must," Mrs. Price murmured and bit her lip. But Chase merely accorded her a nod and led Meredee toward the graves.

Any other time Meredee would have been pleased to show him the area. Some version of St. Mary's had stood on this spot for over six hundred years. The tombstones, some square, some rounded, others cut at an angle like diamonds, crowded the yard. Voices from the departing parishioners came quietly here, like whispers from the past. She could easily point out the tomb of John Travis, one of the surgeons who had attended her father and was much loved in the area, and graves belonging to other friends of her father. But now she kept expecting to turn down a corner and find Algernon huddled against the stones.

Still, she tried, pausing at this stone and that. But Chase seemed no less distracted. His gaze strayed off over the roofs of the town, and his hand continued to rise to his snowy cravat.

"And this fellow," Meredee said, stopping before a well-known stone, "swam the channel in under a minute and established Britain's first colony on the moon."

"Fascinating," Chase murmured.

"My lord, had you some other purpose for this walk?" Meredee asked, hands on her hips. "This tour does not seem to be amusing you."

He quirked a smile. "Forgive me. I had a reason for accosting you, but I'm finding it difficult to concentrate." He tugged at his cravat again.

Meredee peered closer. The bites on his neck were an angry red, and she had to stop herself from reaching up and stroking his cheek in sympathy. "Those bites look fearsome!" she said instead. "I have something that will make them stop itching. I'll send someone up to your house with a bottle as soon as we return to the inn."

"And will this concoction smell any better than the one you used yesterday?" he teased.

Meredee smiled. "That you will have to see for

yourself. It smells like lemon, but I promise you it feels a great deal better on raw skin!"

"So, what is this fellow's true claim to fame?" he asked.

"He was a respected conchologist who corresponded with some of the most noted naturalists of our day." Meredee trailed her hand along the rough stone. "And a beloved father."

He bent down to examine the inscription. "Your father, to be exact."

Meredee nodded as he straightened. "He wanted to be buried in Scarborough. He considered it his home. I suppose I do too."

"He didn't have a house here?"

"Not a permanent one, no. We stayed in inns or, like you, rented a place. He wasn't particular, as long as we were close to the sea and he could further his seashell collection. Now it's mine to care for."

His gaze ventured out to sea again. "A worthy inheritance for someone with an interest in science. My father left Phoebe a considerable sum instead. She will come into it when she marries or reaches her majority. Sometimes I fear that fact influences those who choose to befriend her."

Meredee glanced around for the girl and saw with relief that she was standing next to the carriage, arms crossed eloquently over her chest. "Your sister is so pretty and animated, I doubt anyone looks first to her income."

"And I have nightmares about it," he replied. But he, too, glanced around. "I had something in particular I wished to discuss with you, but it seems we will have to wait. I believe your stepmother has something rather urgent on her mind."

While they had talked, the crowds had thinned until only a few carriages remained in the lane. Her stepmother was a small shadow in front of the church, waving wildly.

"I believe," Meredee said, "that our cart from the inn is ready to depart. I should go."

He caught her hand and held it close. "Ride home with me instead."

He could not know the tremors his touch caused. Yet a part of her longed to spend time with him. She doubted she'd ever get enough of the admiration she saw in his eyes. But she knew she'd never survive a ride home with Mrs. Price and Lady Phoebe both trying to get her attention to discuss Algernon's strange behavior—behavior she still could not mention to Chase.

"I wouldn't want to take you out of your way," she said, pulling back from him. "Perhaps I will see you and Lady Phoebe at the spa tomorrow."

"Count on it," he said. She felt his gaze follow her all the way back to the cart.

Chapter Ten

Meredee finally caught up with her stepbrother after dinner that day. The inn served an Ordinary—a generous meal at two in the afternoon in the private parlor—but Algernon hadn't joined her and his mother and the other guests. Meredee sat where she could keep an eye on the common room outside the open door and sighted him passing just as the innkeeper brought out the final course of stewed apricots and ices. Excusing herself, and earning a frown from her stepmother, she slipped out.

She thought perhaps he'd look haggard from keeping his secrets, but his grin was as bright as ever.

"Where have you been?" she demanded. "You admit you intend to marry Lady Phoebe despite her brother's wishes and then take yourself off without further explanation!"

"Hush!" he cautioned, eyes wide. He took a step

closer and lowered his voice. "This is no place to discuss personal issues. Upstairs."

With a glance over her shoulder to make sure her stepmother was still spooning up her strawberry ice, Meredee hurried after him.

He led her to the sitting room beside their bedchambers. The space was painted a sunny yellow, made brighter by the light from the wide, dark woodframed windows across the far wall. Her stepmother had immediately made herself at home; her lace-making pillow sat on the little half-moon table against the left wall, her cashmere shawl draped the padded seat under the window and her cloak was puddled on one of the spindle-backed chairs that crouched here and there as if begging for guests.

Algernon shut the door. "I meant what I said yesterday. I intend to marry Lady Phoebe as soon as she'll have me."

"Lady Phoebe isn't the one you have to convince. She's only nineteen. You need her brother's permission."

He grimaced and set about pacing the polished wood floor. Meredee sank onto the chair closest to the table and watched. He looked a bit like a stork in his butter-yellow pantaloons and paler yellow coat.

"I'll never get Allyndale's permission," Algernon declared. "He doesn't trust me."

"And why should he?" Meredee rubbed her hands along the pink of her skirt. "Sneaking around behind his back like this. I saw you at services this morning, sir."

Her stepbrother paused to eye her. "Whose side are you on?"

She had asked herself the same question. She had agreed to learn Chase's intentions when she thought Algernon was in danger. Now she had to wonder who was the greater danger—Chase or Algernon. "I remain your devoted sister," she told him, "but I am disappointed in you."

Algernon sighed and pulled out the spindle-backed chair next to hers to seat himself. "Please don't say that. I haven't done anything to shame you."

"Perhaps not, but look what you're doing to the girl you say you love. You are forcing her to choose between you and her family."

"I'm not forcing her!" Algernon leapt to his feet again. "Her brother is the one putting her in this untenable position. Am I such a miserable excuse for a man that he'd refuse to allow me to court her properly?"

"Only you can answer that," Meredee murmured.

He took a deep breath. "I assure you, the thought of marriage makes any man take a good look at himself. I may not have a title, but I'm a decent catch." He ticked off the reasons on his fingers. "I'm from a respectable family; I have a reputation for paying my debts on time; I have a decent income." His grin slipped out. "And I have an exceptional sense of fashion."

Exceptional was the only word for it. Meredee shook her head. "Then why does Lord Allyndale refuse you?"

He threw up his hands. "Because he is a bully and a lout! He insists on controlling every moment of his sister's life, and he will not give her up."

"You mistake him," Meredee insisted. "He loves his sister deeply; I'm sure of it. He's simply trying to protect her."

"From me?" Algernon drew himself up as if affronted. "I just want to marry the chit!"

"Marriage!" his mother cried as she threw open the door and hurried inside. "What's this of marriage?"

Algernon slumped, crumpling his coat and his cravat in the process. "Oh, hello, Mother. Please shut the door before the entire inn hears you."

"Why?" she demanded, but she did as he bid. "They already hear you."

"I certainly hope not," Algernon said, but Meredee noticed that he had quieted his voice.

Mrs. Price picked up her gray skirts and took the chair he had vacated. "What's this about marriage?" she repeated, gaze darting between him and Meredee.

Meredee waited for her stepbrother to speak, but he appeared to be contemplating the curve of one of the filigreed buttons on his gold-shot waistcoat. When the silence stretched, she sighed and turned to her stepmother.

"Algernon and Lady Phoebe are in love and wish to marry," she explained.

Mrs. Price stared at her son. "Is this true?"

Algernon nodded, meeting her gaze at last. "Yes, Mother. But Lord Allyndale has refused us permission."

Mrs. Price straightened. "The arrogance! You're a tremendous catch! You're handsome and clever and well-heeled, and you come from excellent family."

Algernon cast Meredee a look as if to say he'd told her so.

"I believe Lord Allyndale may be looking for more for his sister," she said.

"More?" Mrs. Price looked bewildered. "What more is there?"

Depth of character? Maturity? A willingness to put aside one's needs for another? All of which she feared her stepbrother and Lady Phoebe lacked. But she could not tell him that, especially with her stepmother in the room, without sounding judgmental and ungrateful.

"Perhaps if Algernon were to speak to Lord Allyndale again," Meredee ventured instead. "Explain how much he loves Lady Phoebe."

"He might listen," Mrs. Price agreed. "You do have a way with words, dearest."

"Not when it comes to Phoebe's brother," Algernon insisted. "Frankly, I'd like to carry her off to Scotland to marry. I had it all planned—east to Thirsk, north to Middlesborough, then across to Penrith and up to Gretna Green. I'm certain we could survive any scandal from it. But we could use that dowry of hers." He grinned again. "Phoebe enjoys shopping nearly as much as I do."

Chills ran through Meredee. "Algernon, you are not out for her inheritance?"

"For shame!" Mrs. Price wagged her finger at Meredee. "How can you say such a thing to your brother! After all he's done for you!"

Algernon cocked his head. "Is this jealousy speaking, Meredee? You have neither inheritance nor suitor, so you begrudge Lady Phoebe both?"

Meredee rose on shaky legs. "No! Of course not! But Lord Allyndale is not the monster you painted him. If he's refused you, it's because he has reason."

Mrs. Priced sucked in a breath. "I never thought I'd see the day when a daughter of mine would turn her back on her own family for a near stranger."

"You," Meredee said, gaze blurring with tears, "are not my mother, as you say to total strangers at the least provocation. You asked me to act as your servant and your spy, and to my sorrow I agreed. But this sneaking around is wrong, and I will be a party to it no longer." She ducked her head to keep them from seeing her tears and hurried for her room.

Once inside, she leaned against the door. Algernon couldn't be right. Oh, some part of her longed for an independence, an ability to make choices now denied her. But she didn't begrudge Lady Phoebe those choices. That wasn't why she protested. Love that tore families apart could not be right.

Could not be love.

Certainly there were feuding families who refused their children the right to wed. Look at Romeo and Juliet, and how badly their romance had ended. Surely she was right to caution Algernon against such a course. They were family, and family looked out for each other.

She pushed away from the door and went to kneel before her bed. Lifting the quilt away from the floor, she pulled out the specially designed leather box her father had left her. The black leather was scuffed in places from its travels, and she felt another twinge of guilt when she saw the film of dust on top. Working the brass catches, she lifted the top compartment to fold out first one side and then the other.

The sunlight from the window gleamed on the dozens of shells nestled in velvet-lined compartments. There was the red queen scallop from Cornwall. Each time she looked at it she thought about the time her father had taken her and her mother to that lonely coast and she'd seen the huge Atlantic for the first time, her tiny hand held safely in her mother's.

Then there was the large razor clam, looking like it had been bronzed already, from the coast of Scotland. Her father had found the massive specimen while he and Mrs. Price were on their wedding journey. It was the only shell in the collection that her stepmother was willing to praise.

In the center, a single compartment remained empty. The scrap of parchment tacked to the bottom read, *"tellina incarnata."* Her father's legacy, her life, could be told in these shells. Unfinished. Waiting.

She knew she should have tried harder to find the shell. She should have insisted that they return to Scarborough sooner. But a part of her was just as loath as her stepmother to visit the place again, to open herself to memories that sometimes proved painful. And how could she regret waiting until yesterday to hunt in the North Bay, when yesterday she'd spent the time with Chase?

How he'd grinned through the morning. She still could not believe he'd stayed at her side. A few of her friends had gone hunting with her and her father over the years. They'd never gone more than once, and they'd never stayed more than a few minutes before losing interest and finding better game.

But Chase had seemed sincerely pleased with the process. He'd asked questions about each shell they discovered, and twice she saw him pocket a particularly lovely specimen she knew her father had already collected. He never found excuses to head back to the shade of the trees; he never urged her to hurry. Until Lady Phoebe had disappeared, he'd seemed completely content.

They'd been poking around a tidal pool yesterday

when a thin stream of water had spurted up from the depths. He'd hopped back to save his boots, then peered closer.

"What was that?"

Meredee looked closer, too. Nestled in the little pool were any number of creatures and plants, from the golden flowers of sea mats to clumps of purple coralline algae. A spider crab hurried away from her gaze, as if he had important places to go. "I suspect those are your culprits, my lord."

He gazed down at the cluster of translucent tubes clinging to the darker rocks. They seemed to sway in the breeze, and once in a while clear water shot from the openings.

"Amazing," he said, as if he'd been the first to discover them. "What are these creatures? Have they been catalogued?"

Meredee smiled. "Oh, very likely. They are called sea squirts. They are scraped on a regular basis from pilings and wharves around the Empire."

He chuckled at that. "Well, I still say they look like clever little fellows."

"They are very clever. It takes very little for them to be content. They cling tenaciously to any little outcropping, be it wood or stone or metal, and collect their food from particles in the seawater."

Was that what she'd become, she wondered now. A creature clinging blindly to a family who wanted nothing but to scrape her off?

It hadn't always been this way. When her father had first told her he planned to marry again, to a widow with a nearly grown son, she'd been ecstatic. A family at last! For a time, they were a family. Algernon had always been up for a lark, ready to squire her about. Her father had thought the sun rose and set on him. Mrs. Price had been delighted to see Meredee dressed in the latest styles, to take her to balls and routs, to introduce Meredee to her acquaintances as her husband's daughter. She'd listened at night when Meredee poured out her sorrows about a beau who hadn't come up to scratch and, when Meredee had lost the one man she'd thought she might have married, her stepmother had cried along with her.

And then Meredee's father had fallen ill, and everything had changed.

At first she'd served beside her stepmother because she wanted to be with her father. Then she'd served Mrs. Price because the woman had been even more distraught than Meredee at the loss of Mr. Price. What had started as an act of love had gradually become a duty and then a chore. Algernon and his mother were completely comfortable with the idea that Meredee was meant to serve.

And Meredee hadn't argued. There was comfort in being needed, honor in being useful. She felt rather noble soothing tempers, aiding plans, encouraging dreams. Being helpful was the only reason anyone ever praised her. She'd never questioned that role, until she met Chase Dearborn, Lord Allyndale. She'd packaged her heart in a neat little case, just like her father's shells, safely hidden from the world. Chase had blown off the dust, opened the catches and looked deep inside. Would he see the beauty nestled there?

Lord, show me the way. I feel so lost.

The rap on her door brought her head up.

"Meredee?" Algernon's voice sounded concerned. "Please let me in. We must talk."

"No," she said, closing the case. "We mustn't. Let us merely say that we disagree. You will do as you see fit, and so will I."

"But you won't say anything, will you? You'll keep this in the family?"

A tear slid down her cheek. Perhaps as long as she continued to serve she could at least pretend she had a family.

"Yes, Algernon," she said. "Your secret is safe with me. But be careful. He isn't a man to cross."

"Perhaps you should remember that, too," he murmured.

She needed no reminder. She'd backed herself into a corner with Chase, and she was fairly certain she'd spend the rest of the night worrying about it.

Chapter Eleven

Meredee woke with a start. Golden light glittered through the slats on the window shutters. She'd over-slept!

She threw back the covers and called for a maid to help her dress. In truth, she had spent a difficult night, falling asleep well after the inn had finally quieted. Small wonder she'd slept in. Unfortunately, Mrs. Price would be sure to see this as willful disobedience after yesterday's argument. Worst of all, she'd missed the morning's low tide!

In her cream-colored walking dress with the butter-yellow overskirt, she rapped at her stepmother's door and entered when bid. To her surprise, Mrs. Price was already dressed in a white muslin gown gathered at her neck and cuffs, and sitting up reading a novel they'd borrowed from the subscription library.

"That little maid helped me dress," she explained when Meredee stammered an apology. "She hasn't your gentle touch, but her work will suffice." She set the book down primly in her lap. "We will say no more about yesterday, if you please."

Meredee took that to mean she was forgiven. She could not help wondering, however, whether her stepmother would allow the matter to be forgotten.

She learned the answer the moment they set foot in the spa house later that morning. The day was bright, the air warm. Many of the notables strolled the sands. A few lounged in the cool of the spa house, their conversation a low murmur like the waves. Sir Trevor was promenading about the room, looking every bit the commanding gentleman in his navy coat and tan trousers. Lady Phoebe in a green-sprigged muslin gown giggled on his arm, while Chase watched from near the windows.

Mrs. Price clutched Meredee's arm. "What is that man doing with Algernon's intended?"

Meredee sighed. "Lady Phoebe is not Algernon's intended until he makes his intentions clear to the world."

"And he explained why he cannot do so! Oh, I do not like how she dotes on Sir Trevor. Go interrupt them."

"I shall do nothing of the kind," Meredee said, but her stepmother drew herself up with a hiss like an offended goose.

"Sir Trevor is an old family friend," Meredee reminded her. "I am persuaded Lady Phoebe sees him as another brother."

"We shall see," her stepmother muttered, narrowing her eyes on the pair. "I will not feel comfortable leaving her with the fellow until I am certain. If you will not move yourself for your brother, I will." She released Meredee's arm and stalked across the room, her skirts rustling as if they were every bit as agitated as she was.

"Has my sister done something to offend your family?" Chase asked, strolling up to take Mrs. Price's place at Meredee's side.

She pasted on a bright smile. "Lord Allyndale, how nice to see you."

He bowed. Like Sir Trevor, he wore the navy coat and tan trousers that proclaimed him a man about town. "A pleasure as always," he said as he straightened. "And I must thank you for that ointment. It was very soothing."

"To your skin or your nose?" Meredee teased.

He grinned at her. "Both, I assure you. It was a relief to be able to tie my cravat again."

And rather nicely, too, she thought, noting the more complicated fold. Even Algernon would have approved.

At the thought of her stepbrother, her smile very nearly slipped. Something must have shown on her face, for he took a step closer.

"Is something wrong, Meredee?"

Entirely too many things. She wanted to simply enjoy Chase's company, but thoughts of yesterday's argument with her family kept intruding, as did her realization of how quickly Chase was wedging himself into her heart.

"I'm just a little tired today," she said. "Please think nothing of it."

"You're certain?" He peered closer, and she lowered her gaze lest he see the turmoil inside her. "I intended to wish both you and your stepmother a good morning, but she left before I could do so. She seemed upset, as well."

Meredee glanced up to locate her stepmother. Mrs. Price had stopped Lady Phoebe and Sir Trevor, and engaged them in conversation. At the moment, she seemed quite animated, her hands moving with her words. Lady Phoebe nodded, and the ribbon on her rose-covered bonnet waved in time.

"Is my sister the cause?" Chase asked.

Oh, why had she made Algernon that promise? She'd said she wouldn't betray him, but she couldn't lie to Chase. "My stepmother was concerned that Sir Trevor was perhaps too intent on maintaining your sister's company," she said. "She thought her presence might give Lady Phoebe the excuse to decamp, if she so desired."

His brows rose, and he glanced after her stepmother again. "How extraordinarily kind of her to notice." His look speared Meredee. "Are all the Prices intent on rescuing my sister from her own follies?"

No, my lord, one of them would very much like to encourage her. "Forgive us, my lord. It isn't our place to involve ourselves in your affairs."

"And what if I should ask you to involve yourself?"

She regarded him with a frown. He was watching her intently again, as if the very air he breathed depended on her answer.

"What do you mean?" Mcredee asked.

He glanced at his sister as if to be certain she was in good hands, then offered Meredee his arm. "Would you take a turn around the room with me?"

She ought to refuse. The longer she was in his company, the more she was tempted to blurt out Algernon's secret. Yet his question intrigued her. Why would he want to involve her and her family any more than they already were? He seemed so self-assured, self-controlled. Though he was respectful of people who approached, at church and at the spa, she was certain he gave his confidences only to a privileged few. Was she to be one of them?

Her heart fluttering in her chest, she put her hand on his.

"You have probably realized by now one of the reasons I came to Scarborough," he murmured as they passed several gentlemen seated along the pale green wall. The elderly Mr. Openshaw waved his good hand at her, and she smiled in greeting. "I wanted to provide my sister with a safer environment."

"Safer?" Meredee peered up at his craggy profile. "Was London so very dangerous?"

"For Phoebe, yes. Too many suitors, and too many of them unsuitable." When Meredee frowned, he explained. "Fortune hunters, Meredee. Or worse—those who fancied themselves in love but who lacked the substance to be the husband Phoebe needs."

Algernon came dangerously close to that description. "And Lady Phoebe could not see them for what they were?"

He snorted. "My sister has trouble seeing beyond the next pretty gown."

Though she'd had similar thoughts, she could not help but be disappointed at his sharp assessment of his own sister. "I think you malign her, my lord."

"Perhaps," he allowed. "Sir Trevor offered the same caution. But you will allow that my sister has a way of seeking to gratify momentary interests at the expense of more important matters."

She couldn't argue that, either. Lady Phoebe lived entirely in the moment, with little thought beyond what she wanted right then. "Surely that is only her youth," Meredee protested.

"She takes after our mother," he said. "Lady Allyndale was an ethereal creature, all bright emotion and delicacy. She was a great beauty, and much loved by those who knew her well."

And nothing, nothing like Meredee. Was it not said that men often gravitated to women like their mothers? Why did Chase want to be anywhere near her? She resorted more often to logic than emotion. At the moment, she felt every one of her far-more-substantial curves, the strength of each of her far-from-ethereal steps.

"She sounds delightful," she said, trying not to sigh.

"She was a fragile creature who had difficulty deciding what cap to wear and who worried herself to an early grave. Phoebe is no different. Few of the women I've met are any different. I will admit I despaired for most of womankind, until I met you."

Meredee pulled up short, blinking. They had reached the windows overlooking the sea, and he stood beside her, back to any curious gazes, and brought her hand up to cradle it against his chest. "If I may say, Meredee, I find much to admire in you."

She couldn't speak. The warmth of his gaze, the pressure of his hand on hers, sent her senses spinning. Never had anyone looked at her with so tender a smile. Chase Dearborn, Lord Allyndale, had feelings for her!

Her heart started beating faster, and she waited for the familiar fear to demand her attention. Instead, a fierce yearning rose up inside her. She remembered the giddy days of courting, of holding hands, of laughing over tiny things that meant something only to the two of them. She'd thought those days had died, that a part of her had died along with them. Now here was Chase, offering them to her again, and more. What would it be like to be courted by someone who looked at her so sweetly, to feel his hand in hers, the brush of his lips in longing? To stand before God and His people and pledge their lives, their hearts to each other? To carry his children, to create their own family, people who loved and respected each other?

"You honor me," she murmured.

"You honor me with your friendship," he insisted. "I have never met anyone like you."

Oh, she had to stop him. If he continued like this, she'd either burst into tears or throw herself in his arms, and he'd think her just as emotional as his sister and mother. "Please, my lord," she managed.

But he was clearly warming to his theme. "You are kind, considerate and full of uncommon good sense. Your loyalty, your character are unimpeachable."

Once again, Algernon's shadow darkened her thoughts. She dropped her gaze, trying not to squirm. "I am not such a paragon, my lord."

"In my eyes you are. And that is why I find myself wishing to make you a proposal."

Goodness, he would propose? Here? Now? She found it all too easy to imagine herself saying yes, being enfolded in those strong arms, accepting congratulations from her Scarborough friends. Mrs. Price alone would swoon at the news. Meredee felt like swooning herself.

Oh, Lord, give me strength! Her prayer went up even as her knees started to tremble. She pulled Chase to the side and came down hard on one of the chairs along the wall. "A proposal? Chase, this is so unexpected."

"I realize that," he said, taking the seat beside her but keeping a grip on her hand. "But I have given the matter considerable thought over the last two days, and it seems like the best course of action. Rest assured I will not take advantage of your generosity."

Meredee managed to catch her breath. "I beg your pardon?"

"You are a noble and selfless creature, but I could not in good conscience ask you to chaperone my sister without some compensation for your time."

"Your sister," Meredee repeated numbly. "You're proposing that I chaperone your sister?"

He nodded. "I believe you have much to offer her. Your character, your demeanor, will be a good example to her."

She wasn't sure whether to laugh or cry. What a fool he would think her if he knew where her thoughts had been heading. "So you would rather your sister be like me," she said, unable to keep all the rancor from her tone, "a penniless spinster with little standing even in her own family."

He paled. "Is that how they treat you? You deserve better, Meredee."

And she deserved better than to be forced to serve yet again. Why did everyone persist in seeing her this way?

The greatest of you must be least. I came to serve, not to be served.

The gentle reproof humbled her. Yet even if she swallowed her pride, she knew his suggestion would never work. She pulled her hand from Chase's. "I'm honored you'd extend me such trust, but I fear what you ask is impossible. My stepmother's needs and the hunt for the *incarnata* take up all my time."

"Bring your stepmother with you," he said. "I'm sure Phoebe would be amused."

He truly didn't know much about women, particularly Phoebe and her stepmother, who she suspected were very much two peas in a pod. "Perhaps for the first few outings, but after that I fear no one will be amused."

He chuckled. "You may be right. But Scarborough society is small enough that you should find plenty of opportunity for the two of them to be together and still find ways to amuse, like now." He nodded to where his sister and Mrs. Price were chatting with Mr. Cranell and Colonel Williams. Sir Trevor had taken himself off and was glowering at the group from the far wall. It seemed the handsome baronet was just as protective of Lady Phoebe. Mrs. Barriston evidently found Sir Trevor's attentions interesting, for she was whispering in another woman's ear while both women kept their gazes fastened on him.

"And as for the shell," Chase continued, obviously intent on laying out the benefits of his odious plan, "I believe I have a solution to your problem, as well." He leaned closer, and the scent of sandalwood teased her nose. "What if I were to post a reward for the capture of the *incarnata?*"

This time Meredee did laugh. "Capture? You make it sound like a dangerous animal."

He smiled. "After hunting for it for two days, I can see that finding it will be no easy matter." He reached inside his coat and pulled out a sheet of parchment. "I could send this to the nearest newspaper."

"Wanted," Meredee read when he'd handed it to her, "a seashell of a rare salmon color, long and rounded, in two halves, unbroken in any way. If found acceptable, the bearer will be awarded the sum of one hundred pounds. Submit the shell to Number Four Newborough Street, Scarborough."

"One hundred pounds!" Meredee handed the paper back to him with shaking fingers. "My lord, I cannot accept this."

"Nonsense," he replied, folding the page and slipping it back into his coat. "You will have no need to search for the *incarnata.* It will come to you."

Perhaps, but after what a tempest! "With that

reward, half the town will be looking for it. I shudder to think of the crowds stampeding the beaches."

"The fervor will be short-lived," he assured her, leaning back as if well-pleased with himself. "The *incarnata* will either be found or people will realize it cannot be found so easily and give up the hunt. But I have no doubt with the number of hunters increased your shell cannot escape notice."

"I do believe you think you've considered every angle."

He smiled. "I try, my dear."

He did. She suddenly knew how Lady Phoebe must feel—her life controlled, her emotions swept aside in the wake of his caring logic.

But she was not Lady Phoebe. Hadn't he just praised her for that? Perhaps it was time Lord Allyndale learned just how a less-than-ethereal creature took his high-handedness.

"Your plan is *nearly* flawless," she said and had the satisfaction of seeing the smile fade from his handsome face. "Unfortunately, you have failed to take two issues into consideration."

"Indeed," he said, eyes narrowing. "What would those be?"

"First, the joy of finding the *incarnata* is not in the having, my lord. It's in the search. Though there are markets for rare shells and fishermen always ready to sell what comes up in their nets, my father never bought one of *his* shells. To him, they were only his shells if he had discovered them."

He touched the breast of his coat. "So I'd do you a disserve by enlisting others to find the shell for you."

"Precisely. But I daresay you did it with the best of intentions."

He inclined his head to acknowledge the truth of the statement. "And the second matter?"

That was an even greater miscalculation, but she couldn't explain it to him so easily. Some part of her wanted to help him, to ease his concern that someone would take advantage of his sister, perhaps even to prove to him that his sister—and women in general— were not the feckless creatures he persisted in seeing. Yet she knew what her answer must be.

She rose and dipped a curtsey. "The second matter is my willingness to serve as chaperone for Lady Phoebe. The answer is no, my lord. Thank you for your kind words, but I must refuse."

Chapter Twelve

"What are you thinking?" Algernon demanded when he burst into their sitting room that afternoon, resplendent in an emerald coat and purple plaid trousers. Meredee and Mrs. Price had returned to the inn after her stepmother had finished socializing. Meredee's righteous indignation over Chase's plan had kept her back straight and her gaze unswerving as her stepmother flirted with her elderly swains, but even the kind Mr. Cranell noticed the difference in her.

"Miss Meredee has the most fierce look in her eye today," she heard him whisper to Mrs. Price at one point. "Puts me in mind of an avenging angel. Best to give her a dose from the south well, I think."

She was rather pleased that she'd kept her gaze from seeking Chase's for most of the visit. The two times she glanced in his direction, she'd noted that he was regarding her with a frown and a quirk to his mouth that said he was perplexed. He thought he'd offered her a reasonable bargain. He could not know he'd offered to put her in an impossible position and crushed her hopes in the process.

"My goodness, Algernon," Mrs. Price cried now, dropping the lace she had been working at the half-moon table while Meredee read aloud. "What's happened?"

"Meredee's whistled my prospects down the wind is all," he declared. But he went so far as to shut the door and approach Meredee with more caution, as if unsure of his reception. "I understand Lord Allyndale offered to have you chaperone his sister and you refused."

How had he known? He hadn't been at the spa house, and she hadn't thought anyone was standing near enough to overhear her conversation with Chase. The only other person who might know was Lady Phoebe, if Chase had confided his plan to her. Meredee's stomach tightened. Algernon must still be sneaking around to see the girl.

"Well of course she must refuse," Mrs. Price said with a sniff. "I have far more need of her services than your Lady Phoebe does."

"But that's just it, Mother," Algernon said, running a hand back through his dark hair. "She won't be my Lady Phoebe unless I can convince her to marry me. And for that I need Meredee's help."

"Lady Phoebe seemed inclined to hear your

proposal," Meredee pointed out, laying a ribbon between the pages to mark her place and closing the book. "My involvement hardly seems necessary."

"Her brother broods over her," Algernon protested. "He won't let her out of his sight. Either that, or Sir Trevor Fitzwilliam guards her steps. But if you agreed to be her chaperone, I might have an opportunity to approach her."

"And don't you think that's why I refused?" Meredee dropped the book on the table with a satisfying thud that made Mrs. Price stiffen in her seat. "How can you ask me to put myself in that position? I told you I would not be involved in your schemes."

"But that was before Lord Allyndale offered to involve you!"

"It makes no difference," Meredee insisted. She rose, aware of her stepmother's gaze on her. "My answer is no, and it shall remain no."

She thought they might argue with her, but, to her surprise, Mrs. Price insisted that no more be said on the matter. Algernon stormed out. When he returned for the Ordinary, he cast her glowering glances from across the table. At one time, she might have taken the harsh looks more personally. Now she felt a strength, a peace. *Thank You, Lord, for showing me that my choices are right.*

Her resolve was tested the very next morning. Meredee had returned from a disappointing hunt on the beach and changed into a pale muslin morning dress. As if to make amends, Algernon had left her a new paper by Sir Humphrey Davy about the discovery of a new element, chlorine, and she could hardly wait to read it. She managed to convince Mrs. Price to go to the spa with Colonel Williams as escort and curled up in the window seat of the sitting room to read, pot of tea on the table nearby. But she'd only gotten through the first few paragraphs when a maid brought word that she had a caller downstairs.

Meredee squared her shoulders and rose. It was probably Chase come to plead his case. He'd find her made of stronger stuff.

"Show him up," she ordered.

The maid, a blond girl with a round face and sturdy frame, bobbed a curtsey. "Aye, miss, but it's not a gentleman. It's a young lady."

Lady Phoebe arrived moments later. "Oh, Meredee, you must help me!" She rushed into the room in a flurry of pink and collapsed sobbing in Meredee's arms.

Meredee struggled to collect her thoughts. What could have happened? Had Algernon pressed his case and been refused by Chase? Or worse, had her stepbrother pressured the girl to elope with him?

"There, there," she murmured, patting the smooth back of Lady Phoebe's satin rose short jacket. "Sit down and talk with me. Would you like some tea?"

"Oh, no, I couldn't possibly drink a thing." Lady

Phoebe hiccoughed back a sob, then she straightened to wipe at her eyes with her gloved fingers.

"Won't you tell me what's troubling you?" Meredee murmured, cocking her head to see into the girl's eyes.

Lady Phoebe took a deep breath as if to steady herself and met her gaze with a look of anguish. "Chase says you no longer wish to be my friend."

Meredee recoiled, blinking. "What! I assure you your brother is quite mistaken."

Lady Phoebe brightened immediately, smile blossoming. "Then you will agree to chaperone me?"

So that was the problem. The girl did know her brother's plan. Meredee raised her head. "No, and I do not see how that has anything to do with my friendship for you."

Lady Phoebe regarded her intently, her honey-colored curls peeking out from the edge of her crisp white bonnet. "But it has everything to do with our friendship. Is it that you find me unworthy of your brother, then?"

"Lady Phoebe," Meredee said, putting a hand to a head that was beginning to ache, "my decision has nothing to do with my feelings for you."

"Then why not agree?" she begged.

"You know very well why I can't agree. Algernon would expect me to betray your brother's trust, and I begin to think you would concur."

"Certainly," Lady Phoebe said and went so far as to giggle. "Don't you see? It's perfect!"

Meredee stared at her, hand falling. "Don't you see that it's wrong?"

"No," the girl said. "What I see is that Chase has left us with no other choice."

Meredee threw up her hands. "Then speak to him! Tell him how you feel."

"He has no truck with feelings! With Chase it is all logic and reason." She said the words as if they tasted bad, face scrunched up and nose wrinkled. Meredee wanted to argue with her, but she'd felt the same way yesterday when Chase had made his very reasonable and completely unsuitable proposal.

Lady Phoebe reached out and took Meredee's hand. "But you know how important feelings are, don't you, Meredee?"

Meredee pulled her hand away. Feelings? Feelings did nothing but crowd her, confuse her. Before she knew it, she was pacing around the little room, Lady Phoebe watching her as a gazelle might watch a lion stalk closer. She should probably sit and encourage Lady Phoebe to do the same, but movement eased the tension building inside her. Was that why Algernon kept pacing when he was intent on a discussion?

She had to make Lady Phoebe see reason. Much as Meredee disagreed with Chase at the moment, she knew this reliance on nothing but emotion would only get his sister into trouble. "Sometimes feelings lead us onto the right course," she said. "Sometimes they don't. They must be balanced with other factors—our upbringing, our character, our dreams, our faith."

Lady Phoebe waved them away with one sweep of her pink-clad arm. "Haven't you been in love, even once?"

Her throat tightened, as if even her body rebelled against the question. A memory tugged, one she had been avoiding for days. She'd wrapped it more carefully than her father's shells and put it safely away where it could no longer hurt her. Did she truly want to open it now—in front of Lady Phoebe of all people? But the girl was regarding her with the same intensity her brother so often did, and she felt the same urge to gratify it with the truth.

She sighed. "I thought I might be in love, once. I had a short season when I was seventeen, and there was the most dashing officer—Captain John Metrick of the Nineteenth Light Dragoons."

Lady Phoebe sighed as if she could imagine him in his dress regimentals, standing tall in his blue coat and yellow cuffs, the white braid broadening his chest. She could not know how his smile brightened his dark eyes, made Meredee's heart beat faster.

"I was very taken with him," Meredee told her, "and, I fancy, he with me. We danced at every ball, we talked at every chance. When he held my hand and asked me to wait until he returned from India, I thought my heart might fly to the moon."

"What happened?" Lady Phoebe begged, sinking onto a chair at last. "Did he prove untrue? Did your father deem him unsuitable? Did he and Algernon duel?"

Meredee shook her head. "Nothing so romantic. He never came back. He was killed at the Battle of Assaye."

"Oh!" The girl leaped up and wrapped her arms around Meredee once more.

This time Meredee leaned into the hug. The memory hurt, but she was surprised at how the pain had dimmed. She was no longer the green girl in her first London season, dreaming of what might be. No, fearing that pain, she'd pushed all her dreams into the darkness. Perhaps it was time to bring them back into the light.

"I knew you'd understand," Lady Phoebe said, pulling back. "We none of us know what tomorrow may bring. Look at my father, killed in a hunting accident. Look at Mother, after all her imaginary illnesses, falling prey to a sudden ague. Why, Algernon could be thrown from a horse, drowned in the sea, torn apart by wild dogs in the street!"

Meredee raised a brow.

Lady Phoebe giggled. "Very well, I grant you the last is unlikely. But the fact still stands—while we are forced to remain apart, we are wasting precious time. He loves me, Meredee! You cannot expect me to go about life as if I didn't know, didn't care."

"No, not you," Meredee said with a reluctant smile. "I can see you were never one to wait. So what do you plan to do about it?"

Lady Phoebe set her hands on her hips, fisting her strawberry-colored muslin skirts. "Encourage him! After his declaration on Saturday, I fully expect a formal proposal within the week."

"And then what?" Meredee pressed. "Your brother refused him, and you're not old enough to marry without his permission."

Lady Phoebe narrowed her eyes. "If Algernon proposes—*when* Algernon proposes—I promise you we will be wed."

"Not good enough," Meredee insisted. "I cannot help unless I know all."

The girl squealed and threw her arms around Meredee. "Oh, I knew it! I knew you'd help us!"

Meredee disengaged and took a step back, face stern. "Do not attempt to flatter your way into my good graces. Tell me what you will do if your brother refuses again."

"He won't. Not if you're on our side." When Meredee started to protest, she hurried on. "It's true! He esteems you greatly, Meredee. I'm sure if you were to explain the situation, tell him how much you adore Algernon, Chase would come around."

Would he? He'd said he admired her yesterday, but that was before she'd refused his carefully laid plans. From the beginning, she'd wanted him to like her, first for Algernon's sake and then because she so very much wanted to like him in return. Was their oddly formed friendship strong enough to endure her confession? Her feelings were still in such a jumble that she couldn't trust them any more than she trusted Lady Phoebe.

The girl took a step closer. "He's downstairs right now, waiting for me. I doubt he'd leave me alone with anyone but you. That's how much he trusts you."

Downstairs. Chase was just downstairs. She could go down, make amends, return that intense glow in his eyes when he gazed at her. But was that all she wanted? Was the sum of her dreams now bound around Lord Allyndale's regard? Oh, she couldn't attend to that right now. She needed to focus on Lady Phoebe and Algernon.

"Perhaps we should invite your brother up," she said to Lady Phoebe. "Tell him the truth."

"No, no, silly," Lady Phoebe said with a laugh. "Algernon must propose properly first." She glanced at Meredee out of the corners of her dark eyes. "But if you were to fetch your stepbrother and give us a few moments alone, I'm sure I could bring him up to scratch."

Meredee stared at her. All this time, she'd thought Chase was dangerously close to being correct about his sister. But deep thoughts lurked in those wide brown eyes. Was she the only one who'd noticed?

"You do yourself a disservice, Lady Phoebe," she

said. "You allow your brother to believe you vapid, but you have an intelligence that will not be denied. Why do you hide it?"

Lady Phoebe shrugged. "My mother was one of those vapid females Chase abhors, forever losing her embroidery scissors, unable to remember what she'd ordered for dinner that day. My father's death upset her greatly, I'm told. I was the last piece of him she'd have. Anything I wanted, I generally got, and the very least tantrum served to turn a no into a swift yes."

"Small wonder your brother finds it difficult to admire her."

Lady Phoebe's hands fisted again. "I adored her. She may not have been brilliant, but she was bright and good and everything warm and loving. Everyone expected me to be just like her. Certainly Chase never saw anything different."

"You've never given him the opportunity," Meredee said, hurting for them both.

Lady Phoebe shook her head. "Why should I? When I went to London, it became clear to me that many men are just like Chase—expecting all pretty girls to have a warm heart and an empty head." She laughed, but the sound lacked her usual sparkle. "And I do enjoy being the center of attention, Meredee."

"I imagine many do," Meredee acknowledged. "But I also imagine it's far more satisfying when it's truly earned."

Lady Phoebe relaxed her hands as if with effort.

"Perhaps someday I shall earn it for more than a giggle. Until then, I mean to make the most of it. I've found the most marvelous man in Algernon. He has a fashion sense few can attain. He actually expects me to have an opinion and takes heed of it. He is clever and funny and kind and so handsome he makes my heart beat faster just looking at him."

Meredee spread her hands, smile returning. "Then I suspect I must believe you are truly in love."

Lady Phoebe nodded solemnly. "Oh, I am, I promise you! Won't you please help us?"

How could she answer that? She didn't like Lady Phoebe's duplicity, yet the girl's feelings for Algernon seemed sincere. And what about her stepbrother? Had he fallen in love with the giggly girl or the woman she was becoming?

Help me, Lord. I can't see Your hand.

The door to the sitting room opened, and Algernon strolled in. "Meredee, have you seen…" His eyes lit on Meredee's visitor, and he pulled up short, paling.

"Lady Phoebe," he started, blue eyes widening. "I had no idea…that is, how nice to see you."

Her eyes brimmed with tears. "Oh, Algernon, every second away from you is an eternity."

"Dear heart!" He was across the room in two strides and taking her in his arms. Meredee watched helplessly as he murmured endearing words against the girl's temple. Lady Phoebe closed her eyes and breathed a sigh of pure happiness.

Lord, let me follow Your lead.

"Ten minutes," Meredee said, crossing for the door. "You have exactly ten minutes. If one of you isn't downstairs in that time, I shall tell Lord Allyndale everything."

Chapter Thirteen

Chase sat in the common room of the Bell Inn, cradling his second cup of tea. He was heartily glad he'd decided to rent a house for the summer, rather than staying at a lodging house like most of Scarborough's visitors. For one thing, he liked his privacy. Already he'd had to fend off three well-intentioned requests to play a hand of cards. For another, the innkeeper kept his house remarkably cool. Two cups of his bracing brew, and Chase still felt chilled.

He should probably have gone upstairs with Phoebe, but his sister had begged for a few moments of female conversation with Meredee and Mrs. Price. He hadn't been able to convince himself it was good form to join them.

Truth be told, he abhorred what his sister called female conversation. It seemed to consist of gasps and squeals and whispers and giggles. When he was a child, he was certain the sounds heralded some great revelation to which only his mother and her friends were privy. When he finally insisted on taking his place in the conversation, he'd been disappointed to find that it seldom held anything more weighty than the style of the most recent bonnet to come into fashion.

That was one more reason to admire Meredee. He had yet to hear her resort to such prattle, though Phoebe seemed certain she was capable of it. Still, much as he was coming to know her, he'd misjudged her response to his plan. That frustrated and confused him. Even with her explanation of the need to hunt for the *incarnata* herself, she should have been more interested in chaperoning his sister. Surely she'd prefer the company of people closer to her own age than Mrs. Price and her elderly flirts. Instead of being relegated to the edges of society, she'd be in the thick of things. She seemed to enjoy Phoebe's company. Why refuse him?

As if conjured by his thoughts, Meredee came flying down the stairs in a pale white gown like an angel intent on delivering world-changing news. She paused at the foot of the stair only long enough to spy him in the crowd. Then her gray eyes brightened, and she hurried to his side.

He rose to meet her, setting the cup on the table beside him and smoothing his hands down the thighs of his chamois breeches. His mouth felt suddenly dry. What, was he nervous?

"Good afternoon, my lord," she said with a quick curtsey. "Your sister mentioned that you were waiting. I thought I should thank you for your kindness in bringing her to us."

Chase glanced from her to the now-empty stairwell. "No thanks necessary. But where is my sister?"

"With my…family. She'll be down shortly." She looked to the standing clock near the front door of the inn as if to make certain, then smiled at him. "And how are you today, my lord? Insect bites healing well?"

"I can barely feel the itch." He far preferred it when she used his given name, but he knew she could not do so here without raising questions as to their friendship. But neither could he allow her to stand here in the common room where even now curious gazes darted their way. The private parlor was out of the question, as he could not be alone with her without risking her reputation.

"Would you take a turn with me about the inn yard while we wait?" he asked, offering his arm.

Meredee glanced at the clock again. "Certainly, my lord."

Once outside, Chase's chill abated, though now he felt the dull pounding of a headache coming on. His stomach clenched in protest, but he took a deep breath of the salt-tinged air and forced his muscles to relax. Not every headache meant he was destined to be ill again. He had enough concerns at the moment to give anyone a headache.

"I didn't see you at the shore this morning," he said as they ambled along the edges of the cobbled yard. A large travelling coach was resting near the door, the four black horses rattling their tack and shuffling their feet as if they longed to fly. Grooms and stable boys trotted to and fro carrying luggage, leading riding horses out for other guests. The woman beside him walked calmly along as if they were once more traversing the boards of the spa house and not wandering through barely organized chaos.

"I was on the beach for a few moments," she answered, skirting around a half-empty bucket. "The tide wasn't low enough to do much good."

"Perhaps the afternoon's low tide, then," he offered.

He thought he heard a sigh. "My stepmother intends to find a new book to read," she said. "We'll likely spend the afternoon at the subscription library."

So she truly did dance to the woman's tune. Perhaps she'd been right that adding Phoebe to her chores might be a bit much. Still, he could not quell his disappointment. "Then when do you expect to try again for the shell?"

She rubbed her free hand on her pale skirts. "I cannot be sure. The tides will grow closer together, and less shallow, as the summer progresses. Very soon it will be impossible to find the *incarnata* before fall."

"Are you certain you wouldn't like me to place that advertisement in the paper?"

She shook her head. "No. I told you. If the *incarnata* is to be found, I want to be the one to find it. Besides—" she cast him a quick, unreadable glance "—that was to be my payment for chaperoning your sister, and I refused."

And suddenly, it didn't matter. He wanted to do her a service—find her that shell, capture a castle, defeat Napoleon. "Then consider it my way of thanking you for your past kindness to my family," he said.

"You have already thanked me quite enough, my lord. Please don't place that advertisement. I couldn't bear to see Scarborough's beaches overrun with fortune hunters."

"As you wish," he said. "But you deserve to have that shell, Meredee, if that's what makes you happy."

Her smile was soft and tremulous. "You are too kind, my lord."

"Nonsense," Chase said, her smile warding off the remaining chill. "What did our Lord say? We are none of us truly good."

"There we can certainly agree," she murmured.

He chuckled. "Oh, you'll never get me to agree that you are anything less than perfect."

She glanced at him again, and this time in wonder.

Had no one ever told her how good she was? The same urge rose up, stronger. How could he show her how much he admired her?

"I'll tell you what," he said. "Let's try farther north. What about going up to Whitby later in the week?"

She laughed. "You cannot tour the York Coast for a shell, my lord."

"Why not? Isn't that what your father would do?"

Her lashes, a darker shade than her hair, fluttered down across cheeks sprinkled with tiny freckles. "You are not my father, Chase."

No, and at the moment, he was heartily glad of it, for the feelings rising up inside him were not what a father should feel for a daughter. He was suddenly aware of how close her body was to his, her skirts brushing his boots. Her lips were soft and peachy and close enough to taste.

He forced his gaze past her. "Are you maligning my skills as a valiant shell hunter, madam?" he said, trying for a teasing tone.

"Well," she said, tone matching his, "I do think you might do better if you'd consent to muddy your boots."

"I'll have you know I've had these boots longer than I've known Sir Trevor," he said. "And he's my oldest friend."

"So you've been unfortunate enough to have enormous feet since you were a child."

"Ha! Calumny, madam! I demand a forfeit."

She raised her chin, pressing her lips together as if to hold back laughter. "Nonsense, sir. I thought we'd agreed you still owe me for my many kindnesses."

"Ah, so I did." And all she asked in return was the *incarnata*.

She asks for so little, Lord. Why won't You give it to her?

"Perhaps we could take a trip to one of the more remote bays," she offered as they completed the circuit and started past the door of the inn again. "I've always wanted to try Ravenscar. The name itself is intriguing, don't you think?"

From nowhere, heat rushed up his body, suffocating him. He tugged at his cravat. "It certainly has possibilities. But perhaps we should stay closer to home. If the tides are turning, as you say, our time is short."

She dimpled up at him. "Ah, but if we were both to seek it, how could we fail?"

He smiled at her optimism, but a pain lanced his skull, and he could not stop that grimace that followed.

"My lord, is something wrong?" she asked, hand going to his arm.

Only that he was being baked from the inside out. He might as well face it—he was about to be gloriously ill. "I wonder," he managed, pausing to gulp back the bile that was rising, "if you would mind fetching my sister."

She glanced at him in alarm, then took his elbow and guided him into the shade by the wall. He leaned against the stone, thankful for the strength at his back.

"Stay here," she ordered. "I'll be right back. They should have been down by now in any event."

He nodded, vaguely wondering who else was coming down with Phoebe. The movement set drums to pounding in his head, and he grimaced again. She hurried into the inn.

He closed his eyes and took bracing gulps of the summer air. The voices of coachmen and stable workers seemed to come from a long distance away. He should go to his coach, which was waiting in the lane, but his legs shook so hard he was afraid to take a step lest he fall.

Lord, why? Why are You plaguing me with this illness? The burdens you've given me are not onerous, but there's no one else to carry them. Why make me unequal to the task?

My grace is sufficient for You.

He snatched at the hope the words offered, but his legs gave out, and he sat down hard on the cobbles.

"My lord!" Meredee's cry roused him, and he managed to open his eyes. Her face was white with shock, her eyes like storm clouds about to rain. It hurt thinking he'd pained her. He reached out a hand to touch her face. Beyond her Phoebe had a hand to her lips as if choking back a cry.

"I must be delirious," he said to the concerned faces around him. "I'd swear that's Algernon Whitaker behind you."

And that was the last conscious thought he had for quite some time.

"Chase!" Lady Phoebe cried, kneeling beside him, oblivious to the damage to her pink skirts. Her anguished face cut Meredee to the heart and only spurred the panic inside her.

She'd been right. Chase was ill, terribly ill.

Oh, Lord, please spare him.

She didn't care how impossible the prayer might be, how large a request. She made it with all her heart, with all her will. Chase couldn't die, couldn't leave Phoebe, leave her. She had buried her mother and father, mourned their loss as well as the loss of her valiant officer. She couldn't lose someone else she'd come to care for.

Huddled at their back, the stable workers were whispering, muttering.

"Drunk as a lord," someone said, and there were laughter and sounds of disgust.

"He isn't drunk," she said, frowning at them all. "He's ill. Will someone please fetch his coach? It should be waiting nearby."

"Right away, Miss Meredee," one of the stable lads

piped up and ran for the arch that separated the yard from the street.

"Algernon," she said, turning to her stepbrother who stood there white-faced, "go into the inn and ask Mr. Hollister for a blanket, a damp washcloth and a large bowl."

She was thankful her stepbrother didn't argue but merely ran for the inn, his emerald coat bright against the pale walls.

She gathered up her skirts and crouched beside Lady Phoebe. The girl had finally given up calling her brother's name and now held his hand and wept softly.

"We have to get him somewhere he can be cared for," Meredee told her. "Who is his physician?"

Lady Phoebe looked up. Her creamy skin was mottled with red. "Physician? I didn't know he needed one."

"It will have to be your house, then."

With a rattle and thunder of hooves the Dearborn coach rolled into the yard and turned. Lady Phoebe scrambled up and motioned her coachman and footmen to her.

Meredee took Chase's hand, her own trembling. She put the back of her other hand to his pale forehead and nearly gasped at the heat. Even with his eyes closed, lines of pain bracketed his mouth.

"Lord Allyndale," she murmured, bending closer. "Chase, can you hear me?"

His eyelids fluttered, then opened, and she did gasp then. No light, no reason sat in his blue eyes. The dullness, the lifelessness stabbed at her.

She rallied herself with an effort. "My lord, listen to me. We need to get you home. Can you stand?"

He blinked, then bunched his legs under him and rose, wavering, to his feet. Meredee rose with him, clinging to his hand, ready to put her shoulder to his to keep him upright. She could feel the heat of him, the weakness sapping his usual power. *Fight,* she thought. *Fight hard. Don't give in to this.* Her hand tightened on his until her knuckles whitened.

His footmen slipped in on either side of him. "We have you, my lord," one said.

Meredee released her grip, but Chase's hand turned, grabbed hers, clung to it as if it held any hope of life. Unknowing, the footman took a step forward, and Meredee was tugged with them. She flexed her fingers, but Chase's grip remained tight.

"My lord," she said, bending closer to him, blinking back tears that threatened, "you must let go."

He mumbled something, but then his head sagged forward, and both footmen braced themselves as they took his weight.

Lord, help him!

Meredee pushed away the fears that clawed at her and pulled her hand from his. Wrapping her arms about herself, she stood there, watching, as the footmen carried him to the waiting coach.

Algernon and Mr. Hollister hurried from the inn.

"I have what you wanted," her stepbrother said as he passed her. He strode for the coach, where Phoebe waited for the footmen to lay Chase on the squabs.

The innkeeper handed Meredee a wooden bowl with a damp cloth draping the side and glanced down uncertainly at the plaid wool blanket on his arm. "It wasn't anything he ate here," he said, loudly enough for the crowd's edification.

"No," Meredee agreed. "It's far worse, I fear."

The footmen climbed out of the coach and looked expectantly at Lady Phoebe. The girl shrank back, clinging to Algernon. Meredee shouldered the blanket and hurried to their sides.

"Take him home," she said. She held out the objects. "Here, you may need these."

Lady Phoebe merely stared at her. "Oh, Meredee, I can't do this. I don't know how to do this."

"You must be brave, my sweet," Algernon murmured.

"You must be useful," Meredee corrected. "This is no time to posture! Your brother needs you."

Lady Phoebe shook her head so vigorously she struck Algernon with her bonnet. "I'm not posturing! I don't know what to do! Please, Meredee, you must come with me!"

Chapter Fourteen

Meredee could feel Lady Phoebe's panic, just as she'd felt it the day the girl had almost drowned. Was Chase's sister such an accomplished actress that she could look so afraid, so helpless? If she told the truth, she was incapable of functioning in the emergency. If she lied, she was unwilling to function. Either way, Chase needed someone he could count on to nurse him, and Phoebe wasn't that person.

Oh, how Meredee wanted to be that someone. Though she felt the same fear, she refused to give in to it. She wasn't sure whether she'd be the woman to stand by his side in life, but she could be the woman to sit at his sickbed. Even if God took him home, she would not run from the feelings Chase roused in her.

She turned to the footman, hesitating beside them. "Go to the next street over and fetch Dr. Newcomb." She thought he might refuse—after all, she was hardly his employer. But he nodded and hurried from the yard.

"Inside," she ordered Lady Phoebe, and the other footman helped the girl into the coach.

"Home, Miss?" the coachman asked, touching his tall cap in deference.

"Yes, please," Meredee said before following Phoebe.

Inside, the sight of Chase leaning against the wall of the coach, eyes closed, struck her with the force of a blow.

"What's wrong with him?" Lady Phoebe begged, huddled in a puddle of pink on her side of the carriage.

Meredee draped the blanket over Chase, fingers brushing his pale cheek. "I don't know. But we must do what we can to make him comfortable."

He was sick once on the way to the house. Meredee held the bowl for him and wiped his face afterward. His gaze met hers fleetingly, and she thought he murmured, "Find Trevor," before falling back into a stupor.

"You will not faint," she told Lady Phoebe when the girl started making gasping noises. "I can't take care of you both."

She had a little relief when they reached the house. Lady Phoebe wrung her hands as the footman and coachman carried Chase inside, but Meredee explained the situation, and Beagan, the butler, took charge. Chase was soon resting, covers tucked, in his own bed and gowned in a clean nightshirt with a footman and Valcom, his valet, on hand should he need anything.

"Fair burning up he is," Meredee heard the footman marvel to the valet as he arranged the scroll-backed chairs for Meredee and Lady Phoebe next to the walnut box bed. Unlike the dainty pink room where Meredee had stayed the other night, this room was dark, heavy and masculine, the upholstery, draperies and bed hangings of deep burgundy with gilded iron holding the silk against the walls and edging the walnut furniture. Chase lay before them, his face whiter than the creamy linens. The intensity she found so exhilarating had leaked away, leaving a stillness that shook her. *Lord, please help him!*

Lady Phoebe was chewing on the lace that edged the handkerchief she'd been using to daub her eyes. She hadn't stopped crying since they'd left the inn. "I don't know what's wrong! He's never been sick before."

But when the tall, ascetic Dr. Newcomb arrived and examined Chase, he quickly disabused them of that notion. "Your brother has been to see me twice since you arrived in Scarborough," he told Lady Phoebe when he met with her and Meredee outside the bedchamber. He peered at them both over the tops of his gold-rimmed spectacles. "Apparently, this affliction comes upon him from time to time. I suggested leeches, but he refused the bleeding." He eyed Lady Phoebe. "I do hope you'll be more sensible."

She turned to Meredee, face shadowed in the dim corridor. "I don't know! What do you think?"

Meredee swallowed. How could she make such a decision? Much as she might have wished it otherwise, she had no claim on the man. Yet she'd seen how her father reacted to being bled, growing weaker and weaker until he wasted away. Had Chase feared the same end? Was that why he refused?

"If Lord Allyndale did not think it advisable," she said, "I don't see how we can go against his wishes."

Lady Phoebe nodded, sucking in a breath.

"Then there's not much else I can do," Dr. Newcomb said, irritation evident in his voice. "You might try to force some of the spa water down him. I've seen it help in worse cases than this. Send for me if there's any change."

Meredee thanked him, and the footman saw him out.

Lady Phoebe gasped back a sob. "Oh, what am I to do? I can't lose him! What would I do without him?"

Oh, she knew those feelings. She'd felt that lost. But she was stronger now. She could share that strength with Lady Phoebe.

Meredee met her gaze. "We have to help him. Send

a footman to Mr. Barriston, the governor of the spa. I'm sure he'll send us some of the water."

The girl nodded. "Yes, of course. But you will stay with me, won't you, Meredee? I can't do this alone."

Meredee wrapped her arms around the girl, and Lady Phoebe lay her head on her shoulder. "You aren't alone," Meredee murmured. And neither was she, she realized. She could almost feel the gentle hand on her back, offering comfort, whispering hope.

Thank You, Lord.

She clung to the feeling and urged Phoebe back into the bedchamber.

Someone was trying to drown him. There could be no other explanation for the water clogging his mouth. Chase spat it out, gasped in a breath and swatted at the glass hovering near his mouth.

"Please, my lord, you must drink it!"

Meredee's voice was weary, frightened, and he longed to comfort her. But just opening his eyes was a struggle. Besides, she couldn't be here, in his bedchamber. And why did the footman insist on stoking up the fire? Wasn't it warm enough in here already?

He blinked and focused on the person bending over him. "Meredee?"

His voice came out a dry croak with surprising little volume, but she brightened as if he'd sung an aria. "Oh, Chase! You frightened us so."

The heat was wiped away by a chill that shook him. He'd been ill again.

And she knew.

He struggled to sit up where they'd propped him on pillows.

"No, no," she begged. "Lie still."

He could not let her think he was so weak. He sat, the room swaying around him. He noted Valcom standing against the far wall, his thin face tight and deeply troubled. He at least knew what was happening and liked it no more than Chase did.

"Thank you for your concern," Chase told Meredee, "but I'm fine."

She raised her brows. Her hair had been styled in a braid, but pieces were coming loose and flying about her face like stray sunbeams. Shadows lay like smudges under her gray eyes. How long had she been here? How long had he been ill?

"You most certainly are not fine, sir," she scolded, reaching out as if to put a hand to his forehead. He flinched.

She dropped her hand. "I see. It's my presence you find disturbing. I'm afraid you'll have to make do." Refusing to meet his gaze, she busied herself wringing out a washcloth in the basin beside the bed.

"Where's Phoebe?" Chase asked.

She lay the cloth over the edge of the basin, each move calm and precise. "Your sister is here in the house. She's visited frequently, but she feels unable to act as nurse."

The chill deepened. "And so she forced you to shoulder the burden."

"I was happy to help. It wasn't such a burden." She eyed him and even in his frustration Chase felt the implication. Phoebe hadn't made it a burden; by his attitude, he was making it one now.

He took a deep breath. "We have imposed on your kindness long enough, Miss Price. I'm sure my staff can handle things from here."

She glanced toward Valcom. Chase expected the man to leap forward and resume his duties, but his smile to Meredee showed respect and a reticence to replace her. "Miss Price has been a Godsend, if I may say so, my lord," his valet offered. "A gentleman has to sleep sometime."

"And that's why we have footmen," Chase countered.

Meredee rose and shook out her pale muslin skirts. "Very well, my lord. I will leave you in peace." She paused a moment, lips tight together as if she fought hard words. Then she sat back on the chair and leaned toward him.

"Have I offended you in some way?" she whispered. "Or did I mistake our friendship?"

Chase blinked. "Friendship?"

"Yes, friendship. You escort me to the North Bay, nearly offer a reward for the *incarnata* just because finding it might make me happy, ask to use my given name and say how much you admire my character. I refused to be your sister's chaperone, yet still you persist. What else am I to think but that you wish a friendship?"

Put that way, it was a miracle the woman didn't think he was about to propose marriage. "It is precisely because of that friendship that I cannot have you nursing me like this. It isn't right."

The tension in her face eased. "Friends help one another, my lord."

For one moment, he was tempted. Why not lie back, let someone else deal with his illness, with Phoebe? He certainly could not deny that Meredee was capable. Yet he also could not deny that it was his responsibility, and she had entirely enough on her hands.

"You are too kind," he said. "But I cannot…"

She lay a finger against his lips to stop him. The touch sent a shock through his body, freezing him in place.

"Please?" she murmured, obviously unaware of the effect she was having on him. "Let me do this, if not for your sake, then for Phoebe's."

Her face was soft, her look pleading. He had no trouble refusing Phoebe when she gazed at him that way. Yet he found he couldn't fight, didn't want to fight. He leaned back against the pillows and managed a smile. "I had no idea you could be so determined."

She smiled, as well. "Oh, it is a terrible character flaw, I'm certain." She soaked the cloth in water, wrung it out and placed it gently on his head. The scent of lavender fluttered in her wake.

"Rest easy, my lord," she murmured, and for the first time in a long time, he thought he just might.

Meredee could not feel that determination was such a bad thing over the next few days. From sunup to sundown, she stayed by Chase's side. Either Valcom or Peters the footman stayed with her. The staff knew to call her at any time of the night if she was needed.

She bathed Chase's forehead with cool water laced with lavender, helped him sip of the spa water Mr. Barriston had sent with his compliments and spooned in some of the chicken or beef broth the talented Mrs. Downthistle kept simmering. She read to him from Shakespeare or the Bible. She shared Sir Humphrey Davy's discovery with him. She told him stories of her childhood, half of which she was certain put him into his deep sleeps. She kept Phoebe from smothering him with hugs or drowning him in tears when the girl visited.

She did not think beyond the moment, could not hope for tomorrow. Each second, every breath, was a blessing. Still, she could feel him fighting off the fever, rallying, until on the fourth day she found him cool to the touch and smiling wearily.

Relief was as welcome as warm rain. "I must tell Phoebe," she said, straightening. "And we'll send for Dr. Newcomb, as well." She started away from the bed, but he caught her hand and pressed it to his lips, sending a tingle up her arm.

"Thank you," he said.

Meredee returned his smile. Rubbing the spot where his lips had touched, she went to find Phoebe.

The girl was bent over the desk in the library downstairs, tongue poking from one corner of her mouth as she concentrated on whatever she was writing. She'd visited Chase every morning and afternoon for the last four days but had told Meredee she'd keep herself busy with the household and Chase's estate management. Meredee thought Chase might leap off his bed if he knew, but she was certain the girl was capable of it. Now Lady Phoebe finished her correspondence with a flourish of the quill and glanced up to smile at Meredee.

"The tenants will have new roofs before fall. And how can I help you?"

"He's awake," Meredee said from the door. "And lucid at last. I know he wants to see you."

Phoebe jumped to her feet in a flurry of blue muslin and hurried after her.

Meredee let Phoebe into the room and stopped on

the threshold. Chase's craggy face broke into a grin as his sister launched herself at him. Weak as he was, he still held her gently, murmuring encouragement as her tears began to flow once more. The darkness of the curtained room receded, the candlelight anointing Chase and Phoebe's hair.

That was what family was about—this togetherness, this joy in each other's company. Algernon hadn't so much as showed his face the last few days, and Mrs. Price had sent daily notes demanding to know when Meredee would be free to return to her.

Forgive me, Lord. I don't want to complain. I want to praise You. Thank You for returning Chase to those who love him.

Chase looked up then and motioned Meredee closer. Phoebe patted the chair seat next to hers. They were making room for her, as if she belonged with them, as if she was part of the family.

Emotions tightened her throat, but she hurried to join them.

"So what have you been doing while Meredee spooned gruel in my mouth?" Chase asked his sister with a wink to Meredee that made her cheeks feel warm.

Here was a chance for the girl to confess the good she'd been doing. Meredee couldn't help the disappointment when Phoebe pouted. "It wasn't gruel! It was perfectly fine soup. Mrs. Downthistle added vegetables to it for me."

"Then you haven't been starving," Chase teased.

"Only for company!" She leaned closer and toyed with the satin binding on his blanket. "Now that you're on the mend and my heart can be easy, Chase, you wouldn't mind if I go out a bit, to the spa or the shore?"

He cocked his head. "What about Meredee?"

Phoebe waved a hand. "Oh, she won't mind staying here with you, will you, Meredee?"

And what was she to say to that? On the one hand, Phoebe was once again putting her obligation onto Meredee's shoulders. It had made some sense when Chase was deathly ill and Phoebe was out of her element. It was far less important now that the nursing tasks would be more manageable.

But, truth be told, Meredee would have liked nothing better than to stay. The thought of returning to the little room at the inn, of missing the closeness that had sprung up between her and Chase, made her ache.

Chase saved her from a response. "Phoebe, we have imposed on Meredee long enough. You can't ask her to stay here while you go off to amuse yourself."

Phoebe hopped off her chair. "Well, I like that! You don't want to impose on Meredee yet you gladly impose on me. Am I to have no fun this summer, no moment to myself?"

"It shouldn't be but a few more days," Meredee felt

compelled to put in. "I have a feeling your brother will heal quickly now that the fever's broken."

"A few days!" Phoebe cried. "That's a lifetime!"

"You're being ridiculous," Chase said. "The matter is settled. We will send Meredee back to her step-mother at the first opportunity."

"Very well," Phoebe said, nose in the air, "but you can be certain the first opportunity will be several days from now!" She flounced from the room and slammed the door behind her.

Meredee had risen from her seat to follow, but Chase waved her back. "Sit down, Meredee. She never listens when she's in a pet."

Meredee sank onto the seat. "I'm sure I can stay longer if needed."

"No," he said. "Phoebe has to learn to take some responsibility." He sighed and rubbed the bridge of his nose.

Meredee frowned. "Does your head ache? Dr. Newcomb left a tisane."

"I fear the headache never leaves where my sister is concerned."

"I think you are too hard on her. She's managed the household while you were ill, and she's been dealing with questions regarding the estate."

He closed his eyes. "God help us. The tenant cottages will all be painted pink."

"Perhaps," Meredee said, "but I have it on good

authority that they'll have new roofs before the fall rains come."

"Very likely because the steward suggested it."

"You persist in expecting the worst of her," Meredee protested. "I assure you she's more capable than you know."

"More capable or better at winning hearts? I may have been the son and heir, but Phoebe was the darling, her least wish granted. Father adored her; Mother doted on her. I wasn't much better at first, but I tried to see her educated. I thought surely she'd mature with age."

"She's not so very old. You cannot expect her to grow up overnight."

"Nor do I. But she's had weeks, months, and I see no improvement."

She already felt as if she'd exceeded her bounds in this argument. Yet she could not help thinking that it wasn't just Phoebe he expected to be useless, but most of womankind. Maybe even her. "Perhaps," she said, "you would see improvement if you did not watch her so closely."

He grimaced. "You think I hover? I suppose I do." He gestured down his long form. "I never know when this affliction will strike, and while I'm under its spell, I cannot protect her."

Was this illness the fear that drove him? He had to see that he didn't have to bear it alone. "You have a dedicated staff, my lord. Surely they can see to Phoebe's needs when you cannot."

He shook his head. "It's not so simple. Let me tell you the truth about my sister, Meredee. After all you've done for our family, you deserve to know."

Chapter Fifteen

Meredee stared at him. Chase's face had paled, as if remembering hurt, and he rubbed one hand absently down the soft wool of his blanket. When he swallowed twice before continuing, she reached for the crystal decanter of spa water and poured them each a glass. "It sounds as if you need fortification."

He chuckled. Oh, how she'd missed that sound! "I might at that." He took the glass she offered, held it up in salute and took a deep draught. Meredee sipped hers, the metallic taste strong on her tongue, and made herself sit calmly in the chair. The dark room enveloped them like a cloak. She could hear Valcom behind her, busying himself with Chase's dressing table as if trying not to listen.

"Phoebe first came out a year ago," Chase started. "She no doubt would have come out sooner, but our mother passed away when my sister was seventeen, and we elected to wait a year out of respect."

Meredee felt a smile forming. "You elected, or Phoebe elected?"

He chuckled again. "You know us too well. I elected, and Phoebe fretted. But I didn't think she was ready, and I knew I wasn't. With both parents gone, I had to be part of the whole affair."

"My father hid during the requisite calls and visits," Meredee remembered. "I'm sure most fathers and brothers feel the same way."

"No doubt. But I tried to do things right. We hired a chaperone, a woman of impeccable character; a French hairdresser; and no less than two ladies' maids. Phoebe had enough dresses to gown every young miss in her season twice over. Half of London was at her ball."

It sounded wonderful and awful. She'd hated the balls that became crushes, but Lady Phoebe had probably adored being the center of the feverish pace of action.

"Between Phoebe's natural animation and the rumors of her fortune," he continued, cradling his glass in his large hands, "she was soon besieged by suitors. Several came to beg me for her hand. If I didn't know them personally, I had Sir Trevor investigate them."

"Sir Trevor?" Meredee frowned at him. "Why?"

Chase spread his heads, the candlelight catching on the glass of spa water. "He has connections in a number of circles. There's little that escapes his notice, in society and out."

Was that why the baronet had asked her so many questions the first night she'd dined with Chase? Had she been under investigation? "I imagine some people might take offense," she murmured.

Chase shrugged. "I'd rather risk offense than risk putting my sister into the hands of a wretch. And her suitors proved a lackluster set. I refused them out of hand. But word got out that I didn't wish her to marry. Some took that as a challenge. When I proved immovable, they simply went around me. And I promise you, Phoebe was not nearly as demanding of them."

"Phoebe loves the attention," Meredee allowed. "I imagine it wasn't difficult for them to be encouraged by her."

"So encouraged, one of them tried to abduct her."

She felt as if someone had thrown the spa water into her face. "Oh, Chase, no!"

He met her gaze, eyes hard. "Unfortunately, yes. I didn't see it coming. Victor Delacorte may have been ten years her senior, but he was the second son of a good family. I didn't have Trevor investigate him until it was too late. The only reason I initially refused him was that his older brother felt he was a hothead. I feared he and Phoebe together would be explosive. No one realized he had darker motives in sneaking around with Phoebe. I daresay she found it wildly romantic."

She seemed to find it just as romantic now. What was wrong with the girl that she'd court disaster again?

"But you caught him," Meredee said. She forced herself to relax her grip on the glass. "Lady Phoebe was unharmed."

He set his glass down. "Thanks to Trevor, we caught him before Phoebe even knew she was in danger. He was the one who saw them out in public together. Trevor also learned that Delacorte had lost a considerable sum gambling; he was desperate. He developed an elaborate plan to steal her away while she was walking in Hyde Park and make for the Scottish border. He'd already promised his creditors payment when he returned and used the last of his ready cash to bribe the coachman into looking the other way should Phoebe put up a fight. When we caught him, he had enough laudanum to put an elephant to sleep and a set of ropes to hold her captive."

How horrible! She could imagine Lady Phoebe alone and afraid, calling out for help when none would come. "Small wonder you worry for her," Meredee said. She set the glass on the table lest she do it violence and clenched her fingers in her lap instead.

Chase must have noticed her agitation, for he reached out and covered her hands with his. Under the warm and gentle pressure, her fingers relaxed. It was as if he was protecting her now as he had protected his sister then.

"I worry all the more because we only found out by the grace of God," he said. "Even Trevor wasn't sure what Delacorte planned. But the coachman had a conscience; he came to me with the story. Mr. Delacorte took ship for the Continent rather than face me across the field of honor."

"The duel," Meredee realized, meeting his gaze. "He was the man who fled because of you."

Chase raised a brow and released her. "You heard gossip?"

Her fingers felt cold, and she rubbed them along her skirts. "Someone mentioned you were known to duel, yes."

"I don't make a habit of it. But I will not stand by and see an innocent like Phoebe abused."

"Of course not. But surely not every man who courts your sister is such a villain."

"Not villains, but far from heroes. Her latest inamorata was a fop. He had fewer thoughts in his head than coats in his closet. I didn't bother Trev with investigating him."

She was painfully aware of who he must mean. "Perhaps he had a loyal and kind heart," she tried.

Chase snorted. "His loyalty extended to his tailor and not much else. When he came to profess his undying devotion, all it took was the hint of a duel to send him flying."

"But what did you expect?" Meredee protested, raising her head once more. "You cultivate a reputation of refusal, even vengeance. Of course the fellow gave up!"

"If he truly cared for Phoebe," Chase countered, face tightening again, "he would have stood his ground."

"Outmanned and outgunned? You claim him an imbecile, my lord, but I begin to believe he was a wise man."

He frowned. "You think I was too harsh?"

Would she if she didn't know Algernon? Lady Phoebe had been betrayed, nearly destroyed, by a man who had seemed harmless. How could Chase know that Algernon was any different?

Yet she knew it. Her stepbrother would never hurt Phoebe. Surely he had a right to prove that to Chase.

"I know you did what you thought was best for Phoebe," she assured him. "But perhaps, having once found a wolf in sheep's clothing, you now see wolves grazing with the flock."

He puffed out a sigh. "In truth, I had begun to wonder the same thing. Twice I even thought I saw the fellow here."

"Um," Meredee murmured and reached out to take a long sip of her water.

He leaned back against his pillows. "You've given

me a great deal to think about, Meredee. I appreciate your insights, and your candor."

Meredee rose to let him rest, but she couldn't help smiling wryly. "It's not difficult for me to offer you my opinions, my lord. After all, you can't challenge *me* to a duel."

Chase didn't get much chance to consider his approach to protecting Phoebe. He'd fallen asleep shortly after Meredee had shut the door and, when he woke late the next morning, Valcom stood ready to shave and dress him for the first time in days.

"And may I say what a pleasure it is to be doing so, my lord," he said as he helped Chase pull a shirt over his head.

Even so little a task nearly wore Chase out, but he refused to admit it. "Valcom," he said as his valet busied himself with shaking out a blue satin-striped waistcoat, "do you consider me a harsh man?"

He caught a look of surprise on his valet's face before the fellow wiped clean all expression. "Certainly not, my lord," he said, helping Chase shrug into the waistcoat.

"And would you say anything else if it were true?"

"Certainly not, my lord," Valcom said calmly as Chase turned to face him, but the valet's dark eyes twinkled.

Chase doubted he'd get any more insights from his

other servants. Trevor might feel too beholden to be completely candid. Phoebe, he was certain, would be happy to regale him with his shortcomings. It seemed the only person he could trust to give him an honest, objective assessment was Meredee, and she'd already taken his measure.

He had just settled himself in the library and dismissed the hovering Valcom when Beagan announced Trevor's arrival.

"Come in," Chase called, motioning him to the leather-bound chair next to his. Of all the rooms in the house, he liked the library best. The dark wood paneling and bookcases made the space feel solid, defendable. The hunting scene over the mantel, dusky-green carpet and hint of leather and pipe tobacco reminded him of a gentlemen's club. The crimson drapes were pulled aside to allow sunlight to spear into the room, and a small fire warmed the space.

Trevor moved to join him, eyeing him speculatively. His friend had apparently survived Chase's decline unruffled. His coat was pressed, his cravat crisp and his boots gleaming. "You look as if you're starving for the sight of a friendly face," he said, taking a seat.

"Perhaps not friendly so much as a fellow," Chase replied.

"Bit too many petticoats rustling about, eh?" Trevor chuckled as he spread his feet to the fire. "I tried to come to your rescue earlier in the week, but the dragon guarding your bower wouldn't allow it."

Chase smiled. "Miss Price is determined to see me well."

"I understand, but I had a message that I couldn't entrust to another." He leaned forward, hands on the thighs of his buff trousers. "Delacorte left London three days ago. Odds are he's on his way north, to face you."

The room felt colder, but he knew it wasn't his illness this time. "He ran last time. Should I be concerned?"

"Normally, you're more than a match for him, but after this illness…" Trev didn't finish, but Chase felt the implication. If Delacorte arrived at the door today, Chase would be in no condition to meet him.

"Find out where he is," Chase said. "And keep an eye on Phoebe."

Trevor inclined his head. "My inquiries are already in progress. The local constable has a likeness, and I've dispatched copies to York and Leeds. And I intend to chaperone Phoebe until you're out in society again."

Chase shook his head with a smile. "You're a good man to have as a friend."

He thought Trevor would shoot back a glib reply, but the baronet merely cocked his head. "And as your friend, I need to caution you about another acquaintance of yours—Miss Price."

Chase eyed him. "Explain yourself."

"Do you not find her devotion a bit…excessive?"

His friend hadn't seen him in the grip of the fever. He didn't know how helpless Chase had been, how dependent. Meredee had never made him feel ashamed of his weakness. She'd been patient, cheerful, her whole focus in seeing to his needs.

"She nursed her father for two years," he told Trevor. "She knows her way around a sickroom."

"I've no doubt of that. But why should she serve in yours? Isn't that Phoebe's place?"

Chase snorted. "Phoebe? Do you wish to see me in the grave?"

"No. Nor do I wish to see you leg-shackled to a devious female."

Chase shook his head, suddenly tired. "Miss Price isn't devious, Trev. She has been kindness itself and has never asked the least reward."

"Not yet," Trevor insisted. "But people will talk. Mrs. Barriston has already started her campaign at the spa. An unwed lady, unrelated to you by family bonds, alone with you for days?"

"And me insensible most of the time. I assure you, all my interests were fixed on survival. Besides, we were never alone. A footman, Valcom or Phoebe was always with us."

"So you say, but you also say you were insensible. You cannot know what happened every moment."

Chase raised a brow. "What do you think, Trev, that she stole the silver?"

"Not the silver, but it wouldn't surprise me if her stepmother didn't show up crying compromise and demanding marriage."

Marriage to Meredee? The prospect was not unpleasant. He had no doubt his home would be well run, his least need anticipated. Phoebe would have a chaperone he could trust, a mentor to guide her to maturity. He would have a companion with whom to discuss nature and politics.

"Stop smiling," Trevor ordered. "This isn't amusing! The woman cannot be the selfless creature she seems. No one is that kind to no purpose."

Chase focused his gaze on his friend's face. Trev's dark brows were gathered, mouth in a firm line. "Do you include yourself in that statement?"

Trev met his gaze. "For anyone but you, yes. You know my income comes from selling what I know. I wouldn't be a baronet if I hadn't done my…a person in high position a favor he felt compelled to repay. And the end result was that I had to leave London for a time to avoid the scandal. But that just proves my point."

"What cynical fellows we have become, my lad," Chase said with a sigh. "Is it not possible that someone might choose to do a kindness with no expectation of a reward other than the satisfaction of having been of help?"

Trevor dropped his gaze. "Possible, but, by your leave, unlikely. In my experience, people may be moved to help the less fortunate. They are rarely moved to help their betters unless they expect something in return."

"Not Miss Price," Chase insisted. "I have never met her like."

Trevor narrowed his eyes. "Have you conceived a passion for her, then?"

Had he? He'd wondered what it would be like to kiss her, to press his lips to hers, feel her curves nestled against his body. Yet when he thought of Meredee, he more often thought of simply being together.

He grinned at Trevor. "I cannot say, but there are worse sights a fellow could awake to than Meredee Price bending over him in caring concern."

"Bit earthy for my tastes," Trevor replied, leaning back. "I far prefer ethereal creatures like your sister."

"Ah, is this a request to court Phoebe then?" Chase teased.

Trev held up his hands. "Not from me! I have no wish to end up looking down the barrel of your pistol."

Chase cocked his head. "Even you, Trev? Is my reputation so daunting then that no one will offer for Phoebe?"

Trevor shrugged. "You do make it difficult, old man."

Beagan coughed from the door. "Excuse me, my lord, Sir Trevor," he said when Chase acknowledged him. "Mrs. Price is here."

"I'm sure her stepdaughter will be delighted to see her," Chase said.

A slight movement of Beagan's fingers was the only sign he was in distress. "She didn't ask for Miss Price, my lord. She said she heard you were up to receiving visitors and she's most insistent on seeing you."

Trevor cast Chase a telling look.

"Send her in," Chase said, curious.

Trevor rose. "You have no need for me to watch this."

"Stay," Chase said. "If you're right, I may need a witness."

But he couldn't be right, Chase thought as the tap of Mrs. Price's shoes drew closer. He was surprised to find that his hands had fisted and forced them to release. Meredee Price was no cozening female. He'd have staked his life on it.

Mrs. Price sailed into the room. Her gray hair had been tacked up in some kind of arrangement that was even now falling into her eyes. She kept batting at it with her hand, setting her rumpled gray skirts to swaying. Unless he missed his guess, she was wearing two different shoes.

"So, it's true," she said when Chase and Trevor rose to greet her. "You're up at last."

"Indeed," Chase said, "and thank you for your concern."

"My concern, sir, isn't for you. It's for Meredee."

Out of the corners of his eyes, Chase could see Trevor focused on him again, but he refused meet his friend's gaze. "I assure you she has been a credit to you in this house, madam."

"Certainly she's a credit! Meredee is a fine young lady, dedicated to those she loves."

"Here it comes," Trevor muttered.

"Loves?" Chase pressed, and his fists bunched again.

Mrs. Price waved a hand. "Her family, her friends. Yet you, my lord, have abused such feeling."

Disappointment was so sharp he could taste it like metal on his tongue. Had this illness affected his judgment? Had his family again been betrayed by someone they thought was a friend?

Was the woman he was coming to care for a hideous fraud?

"Miss Price has been chaperoned every minute," Trevor said when Chase remained silent.

"Well, of course she has," Mrs. Price said with a sniff. "I would expect no less."

This time Chase did meet Trevor's puzzled frown before returning his gaze to his visitor. "Forgive me, madam, but I don't understand your purpose in coming here."

"I'm here," she said, hands on her hips, "because I want Meredee returned to me. I cannot find my belongings. Simply look at the wreck those girls at the inn made of my hair! You must release my daughter to me at once, sir! I need her more than you do!"

Chapter Sixteen

Meredee was walking with Lady Phoebe in the little walled garden behind the house when the footman came to tell her her stepmother was waiting. The sun warm on the back of her butter-yellow short jacket and damask roses scenting the air had lifted her spirits, and she fancied Phoebe looked happier, as well. She purposely hadn't raised the subject of leaving. Part of her feared Phoebe's reaction, but the larger part feared her own.

"Tell her you're needed here," Lady Phoebe insisted, following Meredee along the graveled path toward the house. Bright flowers and dusky shrubs clustered on either side, and a bee buzzed past. "We simply cannot get on without you."

"That's not true," Meredee started, feeling obliged to argue with the girl. Then inspiration struck. Between Lady Phoebe and Mrs. Price, who would come out the winner in a contest of wills?

"But by all means," Meredee continued, "come discuss the matter with her yourself."

Lady Phoebe nodded. "Assuredly! I'd be delighted to make my case. I'm sure your stepmother will be accommodating."

Meredee smiled at that, and the two of them started for the house again. A sharp hiss from the shrubbery drew them up short.

Meredee groaned. "I recognize that crimson coat, sir."

Algernon slipped into the sunlight. "Are you implying I wear the same coat too frequently, madam?"

"No, no, Algernon, of course not," Phoebe cried as if Meredee had maligned his very character.

"Your coat is not the issue," Meredee said, gaze darting toward the house. "Your presence is. Lord Allyndale is up and about today. You cannot be seen."

"Then go and keep him entertained," Algernon said, taking Lady Phoebe's hand and threading it through his arm. "I wish to have words with the most beautiful girl in Scarborough."

Lady Phoebe giggled, but Meredee affixed him with such a look that he instantly lowered his gaze.

"Forgive me. I didn't mean to order you about."

"But you will help us, won't you, dear Meredee?" Lady Phoebe said. Without waiting for an answer, she tugged Algernon farther away from the house.

Meredee shuffled back and forth on her feet a moment, skirts swinging. Should she follow them, pull Lady Phoebe back to the house? Somehow she thought the girl would put up a fuss. But Meredee couldn't bring herself to carry the tale to Chase like some gossip. And then there was her stepmother, demanding her presence. She put a hand to her head and hurried for the house.

She pulled up short when she found Chase waiting for her just down the corridor. He was leaning against the paneled wall and even in the dim light she could see that he had paled. Her fears for Algernon instantly evaporated.

"My lord," she cried, rushing to his side. "You should be sitting down."

He managed a smile. "Nonsense. I must push myself if I'm to recover." He lowered his voice. "I wanted to talk to you before you met with your stepmother. She wishes you to return to the inn immediately."

Meredee's heart plummeted. She wanted to dig her fingers into the folds of his navy coat, refuse to let go. For a moment, in this house, she'd felt truly needed, truly wanted. But this was not her home, and she had a duty to her family.

"Then I suppose I had better go gather my things," she said, holding herself stiffly.

"We have been through a great deal, you and I," he murmured, watching her. "It emboldens me to ask an impertinence. When you return to the inn, will it be as a servant to Mrs. Price?"

She should deny it. She had some pride. But he had allowed her to shoulder his weakness. Could she do any less?

"In essence, yes," she admitted, then hurried on. "But you mustn't think badly of her. It's just her way."

"And have I been any better?" He took her hand and intertwined their fingers. The brush of his skin against hers sent tremors through her, but she couldn't pull away from the warmth.

"You were ill," she murmured. "You needed me."

"I begin to think I always will."

Meredee's breath caught. She could barely look at him, afraid to find she was wrong yet again. "You are too kind."

"Kindness has nothing to do with it. Tell me, Meredee, would you prefer to stay a while longer?"

Nothing would have pleased her more, but she couldn't. Oh, she couldn't. He was well enough that he no longer needed a nurse. She had no reason to linger.

"I cannot stay. Please don't ask me. We both know it would be unseemly."

"I could have a relapse."

She squeezed his hand. "Don't say that." Meeting his gaze, she saw his grin and blushed. "That's quite enough, sir! The Lord may see fit to grant that petition, and what would we do then?"

"Continue as we have, with you reading me love poetry."

"Oh! I'm certain I never …"

"'Shall I compare thee to a summer's day,'" he quoted. "'Thou art more lovely and more temperate.'"

"I most certainly never read you that!"

"Perhaps I dreamed it then. Or perhaps I should read it to you."

She did not understand his mood. His mouth quirked as if he joked, yet the intensity of his blue gaze was serious, commanding. "I wish you wouldn't tease me," she murmured. "If you have something to say, say it outright."

She nearly cried out when he released her hand. "May I call on you at the inn?"

"Yes, of course! Oh!" And run into Algernon? How was she to prevent that?

"Oh?" He cocked his head. "Is there some reason you'd prefer I stay away?"

Never! Against all odds, against all reason, he wanted to call on her, perhaps to court her. She might have a chance at a future with this wondrous man. How could she refuse him? Yet how could she chance him running across her stepbrother?

She squared her shoulders. "No reason, my lord, expect a minor impediment I am assured will resolve itself shortly. I should be delighted to receive you whenever you choose to call."

He brought her hand to his lips and pressed a kiss against it. She closed her eyes, allowing herself merely to feel for a moment, to breathe against the sensations rushing through her.

"Tomorrow afternoon, I think," he said, and she opened her eyes to find him smiling at her. "If I'm not well enough by then, you'll simply have to return to nurse me."

"Either way, then," Meredee said, returning his smile, "I will see you tomorrow."

"You have been terribly missed," Mrs. Price lamented as their coach carried her and Meredee back to the inn. "I could not get the inn wife to understand how I like my eggs, and no one knows how to soothe my headaches as you do."

Once she would have been pleased to know she had been so helpful. Now she merely wanted to sit and dream of what might be. She could imagine herself walking the sands with Chase, attending the assembly on his arm, sitting across the table from him at dinner speaking of science, of philosophy.

Oh, Father, I never knew how much I wanted these things. Is it wrong? I thought I understood the path You wanted for my life. Now I want more.

Her stepmother was happy to prattle on, barely pausing on occasion for Meredee to murmur agreement. Mrs. Price didn't seem to notice any change in her stepdaughter. Meredee could only wonder why it wasn't written on her face, shining from her eyes.

She was in love with Chase Dearborn, Earl of Allyndale.

And he might, oh he might, be in love with her! How could she sit still? She wanted to dance about the little sitting room, throw her hands up in the air, twirl in a circle of joy.

Mrs. Price, however, seemed determined that the world progress as it always had. She sat in her chair by the table and took up her lace pillow again. The book Meredee had been reading sat in the same place at the end of the table; the ribbon marked the same page.

The room suddenly felt small, cramped. She needed air.

"When do you expect Algernon to return?" Meredee asked, wandering to the window and gazing out at the rear yard of the inn. Beyond her, houses rose to the top of the hill, the creamy walls gleaming in the summer sun. Still the feeling of being trapped persisted.

"I'm sure I couldn't say," Mrs. Price replied with a shake of her head. "He's been cavorting all over town while you've been gone, on occasion with his intended."

Meredee turned with a frown. "With Lady Phoebe? I had no idea she'd left the house."

"Not that easy to chaperone a young girl, is it?"

Mrs. Price said, levering her needle at Meredee. "You can be sure she was careful to slip away unnoticed. Clever girl, I'll give her that."

Clever, but certainly not thinking clearly. Did she truly believe someone wouldn't mention her behavior to Chase? Or was the girl trying to force a confrontation between her brother and Algernon?

"And Algernon?" Meredee asked, crossing to the table. "Is he happy with these arrangements?"

"As happy as may be," Mrs. Price replied, threading the needle once more through her pattern and drawing the thread tight. "I do believe he intends to offer for Lady Phoebe as soon as her brother is well enough to receive him."

Relief, like a draught of cool water, washed over Meredee. No more skulking around! No more half-truths. "Oh, that would be wonderful!"

"I suppose." Mrs. Price heaved a sigh and started another row. "Though what is to become of us I'm sure I don't know."

Meredee perched on the chair with a frown. "What do you mean?"

"Well, I very much doubt Algernon's wife will want two other women hanging about. Depend on it—she will insist that we find alternative lodging. Your father left him the town house, you know."

Of course, she knew that. She'd simply never considered the ramifications of Algernon marrying. Her home, gone? Her room, belonging to someone else?

What of her father's library, the books and books of literature, science, history and philosophy? Was she never to read them again?

She must have looked as stricken as she felt, for Mrs. Price stuck her needle in the lace pillow and reached out to pat her hand. "There, now—never fear. We will always have each other."

That prospect did not seem so very encouraging at the moment. But her stepmother was right—Lady Phoebe of all people would not stand to have anyone else but her run her household.

"But what if I marry?" Meredee asked, gaze rising.

Mrs. Price removed her hand and trilled a laugh. "You, marry? Once perhaps, but you are firmly on the shelf now, my dear."

The words would have hurt a great deal more a few days ago. Now she wanted to shout—*You're wrong! He loves me!* But Chase hadn't said those words, had made her no promises, so she didn't dare confess her hopes.

"Though I suppose I may find a suitable match myself," her stepmother continued, oblivious to Meredee's roiling emotions. "Colonel Williams has been most attentive." She patted her gray curls.

Meredee couldn't stay in this room another minute without bursting out in some inappropriate comment. She rose and shook out her skirts. "I believe the tide will be at its lowest in a quarter hour this afternoon.

If you'll excuse me, I should see if I can find Father's shell."

"What?" Mrs. Price hopped to her feet, tumbling her pillow to the floor. "No! You've only just returned to me, and I will not have you running off again, particularly for so feeble a reason."

"Do you intend to make me a prisoner, then?" Meredee asked, struggling with her temper. "It seems you have already determined to make me a slave."

"A slave! Well, I never!" She sank back onto the seat, face crumbling, lips quivering. "Go, then," she said with a wave of her hand, gaze on the tabletop. "Go chase your shells. I'm sure they mean much more to you than I do."

Meredee was tempted. Fears and hopes crowded her in equal measure. After dealing with Lady Phoebe, she was fairly sure that at least part of her stepmother's lamenting was posturing meant to manipulate her. Yet one look at the tears trickling down her stepmother's soft face, and she knew it wasn't all posturing. She knelt on the floor and took her hands.

"Dearest, you know I care for you. When Father brought you home, I was the happiest of girls because I was to have a mother again."

Mrs. Price sighed. "I was never old enough to be your mother, but those were good times. How lovely you looked at your come-out. Your father and I were so proud." She sucked back a sob. "But then it was all ruined! Why did he leave us with no security? Why do all my husbands disappoint me so?"

Was that why her stepmother clung so tightly to the pursestrings, why she clung so tightly to Meredee? She was afraid of being destitute, being alone. Meredee knew those same feelings. She'd lived through them with her mother's death, her captain's death and her father's. Each time, she was certain she'd never recover from the blow. Each time, she'd risen, stronger.

You got me through those times, Lord. Forgive me for not seeing it until now.

"You are not alone," she said, squeezing her stepmother's hands. "And Algernon would never let you starve."

"Not intentionally," her stepmother agreed. "But he is not the most dependable of sons. I never know when he'll take some maggot in his brain. Just look at that hideous red coat he insists upon. He looks like he should be riding to hounds or marching in the infantry!"

"He simply has his own sense of fashion," Meredee protested.

"And is it any better than a child's?"

She could not answer that question. She wanted to believe that her stepbrother had grown up and was ready to shoulder his responsibilities, to his mother, to his wife, to her.

"He cannot remain a child," Meredee said, "if he plans to marry and raise a family."

"A family that does not include us. We'll be left to fend for ourselves." She pulled her hands away and cupped Meredee's face, fingers gentle against her skin. "Do you see why I dote on you? Two husbands buried, a son I dare not lean on? You are the only reliable person around me, Meredee. I do not know how to get on without you! So please, no more talk of slaves. If anyone in this family is trapped in a life she did not choose, I fear it's me."

Meredee wrapped her arms around her then and held her while she cried out her concerns. The knowledge that her stepmother's harsh words and unkind actions were driven by fear made them easier to forgive. Yet surely forgiveness was not enough. Her stepmother needed assurances that she'd be cared for, that, whatever happened, she was loved.

Never will I leave you, never will I forsake you.

"You are not alone," Meredee repeated. "We will determine the future together."

Her stepmother sniffed. "Even if you marry?"

Meredee's arms tightened. She could not speak for Chase, yet she was certain that, if he loved her, he'd find some way to settle her stepmother. Lord knew he had enough experience dealing with the temperamental Phoebe.

"Even if I marry," she promised. "And I will speak to Algernon. He holds all our futures in his hands—yours, mine and Lady Phoebe's. He must be made to live up to his responsibilities."

"And if he won't?" her stepmother asked, raising her head.

"If he won't listen to me," Meredee said, determination building, "I may know the very person he will not dare to cross."

Chapter Seventeen

Chase went to sleep early that night. He had expected to be exhausted after his first day up, but, in truth, it was not weariness that drove him to bed. Trevor had come to escort Phoebe to the Assembly Rooms for the evening, and Chase could feel the house around him, quiet, empty.

Lonely.

He had never thought of himself as a lonely man. He kept busy attending to his estate, his duties in Parliament and Phoebe's needs. He generally found time to ride, to read, to attend the occasional opera. But until this illness, he'd never realized how pleasant it was to have someone else who could share those duties and pastimes, provide opinions or simply listen to him as he developed his own.

He'd never realized how much he needed someone like Meredee.

No, not someone like her, he corrected himself

as he lay on the bed, gaze on the underside of the box bed's canopy. What he needed *was* Meredee. She was intelligent, she was caring. She consistently, relentlessly put others before herself. It was a trait he knew the Lord intended for all His followers, yet she seemed to embody it more than anyone he'd ever met.

Moreover, she made life interesting and far less vexing. She was calm, she was capable, yet always beneath her exterior was the hint of amusement. Her peachy lips would quirk whenever Phoebe said something absurd, whenever Chase became too entrenched in his opinions. He had never really listed the attributes he sought in a bride, but he wasn't surprised to find that, when he considered the matter now, Meredee held every one.

The question then was what he intended to do about it.

He was still ill, despite daily doses of the so-called miraculous spa waters. Perhaps he'd always be ill. He'd been afraid to trust anyone with the secret, but Meredee had dealt with the situation with laudable aplomb.

Phoebe was still Phoebe, with all her demands and chaotic moods. Yet she seemed better with Meredee, more focused, more easily encouraged to better behavior. And, even when Phoebe was behaving at her worst, Meredee had a way of keeping the situation from becoming explosive.

So, could he do it? Could he marry now, despite his family issues and his health?

Only to Meredee.

He closed his eyes. He'd ask her tomorrow when he visited. He liked to think he wasn't a vain man, but the look in her eyes when she gazed at him, her breathlessness when their hands touched, told him she admired him. And he certainly offered her more than her stepmother ever could.

He would propose, Meredee would agree and they would make plans for their future. And if she fell into his arms for a few moments in between, well, that was only to be expected. The thought allowed him to drift off to sleep with a smile.

Algernon did not go to bed nearly as early. Though Meredee waited up for him, he came in after she'd fallen asleep in the chair. Though she woke early with a crick in her neck, he had already gone out.

"I begin to think he's avoiding us," Meredee complained to her stepmother over breakfast in the sitting room after she'd had the maid help her into her white muslin gown with the embroidered yellow overcoat.

"He cannot do so for long," Mrs. Price assured her, pouring herself a cup of tea. "I'm sure in the next day or so, we shall bring him to ground."

Meredee set down her own cup. "We must find him today. Lord Allyndale said he would visit this afternoon. With no warning, Algernon could well be here when he arrives."

Mrs. Price paled. "And they could duel! Oh, my poor boy!"

"We will scour the town," Meredee promised. "Scarborough is not so large that Algernon can escape us."

Indeed, they heard word of Algernon the moment they set foot in the spa house a short while later.

"Mr. Whitaker is a very interesting gentleman," Mrs. Barriston interjected when Meredee asked another woman about her stepbrother. The dark-haired wife of the governor of the spa narrowed her eyes as if she had sighted her quarry. "He and Lady Phoebe Dearborn make a very attractive couple. Shall we be hearing more soon?"

"La, who can say?" Mrs. Price returned with a panicked glance to Meredee.

"You might caution him that he is not alone in appreciating Lady Phoebe's charms," Mrs. Barriston advised. "Sir Trevor Fitzwilliam has been most attentive of late, and only this morning a Mr. Victor Delacorte from London asked after her."

Meredee felt as if the air had thinned. "Victor Delacorte? You're certain?"

Mrs. Barriston raised her dark brows as if astonished that anyone would question her knowledge. "Of course I'm certain, Miss Price. A fine-looking man with exceptional manners, unlike some I could name."

Meredee ignored the barb. "Have you told anyone else—the earl? Sir Trevor?"

The governor's wife pointed her long nose at Meredee, eyes lighting. "No. Should I?"

"Assuredly!" Meredee met her gaze. "If you see Lord Allyndale or his friend, you must tell them, Mrs. Barriston. This is one story they would greatly appreciate."

"What are you doing?" Mrs. Price whispered as Meredee grabbed her arm and hurried her away. "Why encourage her to gossip? Who is this Delacorte fellow?"

"I cannot explain," Meredee said, steering her toward the path to the beach. "Suffice it to say that now it is even more important that we find Algernon and Lady Phoebe."

Mrs. Price clutched her beaded reticule in front of her blue-striped walking dress. "But I thought you wished Lord Allyndale to know about this Delacorte. Shouldn't we tell him first?"

Meredee stopped so quickly her stepmother stumbled past her. What should she do? Chase needed to know that Victor Delacorte was in Scarborough and asking after Phoebe. But if Phoebe's previous swain found her first, who knew what kind of trouble he'd cause? Chase was in no condition to stop him, but she didn't like thinking what would happen if Algernon tried.

Sending up a quick prayer for help, she took a deep breath. "Algernon must be our first concern," she said when her stepmother eyed her, clearly confused. "Very likely he is with Lady Phoebe. If we find him, we can warn them both."

"Warn them about what?" Mrs. Price demanded, but Meredee set off once more, and she could only follow.

The sands were thronged with promenading fashionables, but though Meredee and Mrs. Price nodded greetings and hurried along, they caught no sight of Lady Phoebe or Algernon. Each person they passed, each parasol they peered under, Meredee's fears rose. Where could Algernon be? Had Delacorte accosted Lady Phoebe?

At the end of the promenade, Meredee stepped back up onto the pavement at the edge of the harbor and craned her neck. It should have been easy to spot a bright coat among the more traditional navy and green and tan. If nothing else, she would know Lady Phoebe's giggle a mile away.

Lord, help us! We only want to keep them safe!

"Mrs. Price, Miss Price," Sir Trevor called in greeting, strolling up to them and tipping his high-crowned beaver with a ready smile that revealed a dimple in his square-jawed face. "And where are you lovely ladies heading this fine day?"

She very nearly hugged him. Instead, she affixed her stepmother with a determined glare. "Wait here."

Mrs. Price opened her mouth in an O of surprise, but Meredee grabbed the sleeve of Sir Trevor's dove-gray coat and pulled him away from her stepmother up the street. "There's no time for an explanation," she said. "I understand you know the story about the Dearborns and Victor Delacorte."

All affability fled. He jerked her to a stop. His chin came down, his stance widened and his green eyes were chips of jade. "How do you know that story?"

He obviously expected her to cower; she refused. "Lord Allyndale told me. I just learned that Delacorte is here, in Scarborough. He was asking after Lady Phoebe at the spa this morning."

His dark brows gathered. "He's asking after Lady Phoebe? Not Lord Allyndale?"

Meredee nodded. "I've been trying to find her to warn her."

"What a kind soul you are to be sure." There was no warmth to the praise. "But why did you have to search for her? She left the house earlier today while I was exercising my horse. I was certain the staff said she had gone to visit you."

Meredee shook her head. "I knew nothing of a visit. We left the inn earlier this morning for the spa."

"So you wish me to believe that Lady Phoebe is

wandering around Scarborough alone, with Delacorte on the loose?"

The thought sent a shiver through her. She could not let him carry such a tale to Chase. "No. I have reason to believe she's escorted by a gentleman named Algernon Whitaker."

His laugh sounded forced. "The day could not get better. Do you know Whitaker?"

"Yes," Meredee admitted cautiously.

"Good. Find him. Bring him and Lady Phoebe back to the Dearborns' house. Leave Delacorte to me."

By the glint in his eye, she thought Algernon had gotten off easy.

"What was that about?" Mrs. Price asked when Sir Trevor had strode off up the street.

"The baronet is going to help us," Meredee replied, leading her stepmother in the opposite direction.

Mrs. Price smiled coyly, glancing back at him over her shoulder. "Well, of course he is. I knew that boy was fascinated with me. After all, he recognized how much we look like sisters!"

They tried the shops next, then the Assembly Rooms on Long Street. In both places, they encountered acquaintances who had seen Algernon, but not recently. And more than one wished to know if they might expect to hear an announcement about him and Lady Phoebe.

"At this rate," Meredee told Mrs. Price as they left,

"his friends in London will know his intentions before Lord Allyndale!"

"What can he be thinking?" Mrs. Price wailed. "If merely asking in private to court the girl gained him an invitation to a duel, what good can come from pursuing her in public?"

"He's trying to force Lord Allyndale's hand," Meredee guessed. "If the entire town expects a marriage, he thinks Lord Allyndale will not dare refuse him. But he severely underestimates the earl's determination to protect his sister."

And he could not know how much Phoebe needed protection. Meredee could appreciate why Chase felt so frustrated with the girl, for she was equally frustrated with Algernon. She wanted nothing so much as to shake some sense into her stepbrother. He might not know that Delacorte posed a danger, but had Algernon no thought as to what would happen if he failed to gain Chase's approval to marry Lady Phoebe? Her reputation was sure to be damaged. And he could have no way of knowing that he was threatening Meredee's future, as well. She had no doubt that if Chase discovered Algernon before her stepbrother professed his intentions, Chase would wish both Algernon and Meredee to perdition.

And they would deserve it.

What had started as a way to protect her stepbrother had become a horrid game she had no wish to play. If her stepbrother could not be found, or worse, could not be made to see reason, she would tell Chase herself when he came calling later this afternoon.

The very thought of telling him hurried her steps and knotted her stomach. She thought their discussion about his rejection of Lady Phoebe's suitors had given him a new perspective. But how would he react knowing she'd kept Algernon's presence in Scarborough a secret from him, especially now that the secret might be putting Phoebe's future in danger?

"Will…you…slow…down?" Mrs. Price panted, hand on her side as if she nursed a stitch. "Never… find him…at this rate."

Meredee stopped and apologized and let her stepmother catch her breath.

"I'm fine," she insisted with a wave when Meredee expressed concern. "But I could cheerfully strangle Algernon for this. He owes me a new pair of shoes!"

"There is one other place we could try," Meredee ventured. "I doubt he'd take Lady Phoebe there, but they may know his direction."

But even Algernon's tailor, when they ventured into that hallowed establishment, had no idea how to find him.

"Though I am told," the tall elegant tailor said with a smile, "that I may shortly have the honor of creating a wedding suit for Mr. Whitaker."

Meredee pulled Mrs. Price out of the shop before he could question them.

"We should return to the inn," Mrs. Price insisted. "He must come home to dine."

But the bell for the Ordinary sounded promptly at two, and still her stepbrother stayed away. Meredee barely tasted the salmon with dill sauce and the cold roast beef.

She was going to have to tell Chase herself.

She waited on the hard-backed chair in the sitting room. The clock downstairs chimed the hour. She felt as if it tolled her doom. Every hope, every dream, was about to be dealt a death blow. Algneron and Lady Phoebe could be in danger at that very moment. And she had no idea how to stop it.

Mrs. Price, who had been working on her lace, set the pillow on the table. "I shall stay with you when he comes."

Meredee shook her head, the movement painful, as if her whole body was encased in lead. "No. If he's going to be furious, I'd rather you not witness it."

Mrs. Price's eyes widened. "Do you think he would do you a violence? Refuse to see him!"

"You mistake me. I believe he will say nothing I do not deserve to hear. I'd simply prefer to hear it alone."

She thought her stepmother might argue, but Mrs. Price nodded and returned to her work. "Just remember," she said, weaving a line of thread with her needle, "this is all Algernon's fault. If he cannot be bothered to clean up his own mess, I see no reason why you should."

Meredee raised her brows. "You surprise me. I thought surely you'd advise me to protect Algernon at all costs."

She snipped off a thread with little silver scissors. "Algernon has not shown himself capable of putting my needs first. You are rather good at that. Of course I must favor you in this instance."

"Of course," Meredee said with a wry smile.

She nearly jumped off her seat when, a few moments later, a servant rapped on the door and opened it to admit Chase.

She drank in the sight of him. She fancied there were a few more lines on his craggy face, but they only lent it a greater distinction. He stood tall, strong, his blue eyes bright, his sandy-haired head high, every bit the earl. She wanted to reach out, gather him close, memorize the scent of him, the feel of him.

Would this be the last time she saw his smile? The last time he bowed over her hand? The soft pressure on her fingers made the words stick in her throat.

"I believe I'll go fetch some tea," Mrs. Price said after greeting him. "I'll be back shortly." She hurried from the room with a last look at Meredee, as if she expected to find her missing some part of her body when she returned.

Meredee expected it as well; she expected it would be her heart that would be broken.

"Have you seen Sir Trevor?" she asked before he could sit.

He frowned as if surprised by the question, then laid his tan driving gloves on the table along with his top hat. "Not since this morning when he went for a ride."

There went one chance he might already know. She tried another tack. "And your sister?"

His frown deepened. "She is here with you, is she not?"

Meredee thought she might be ill. "When did she tell you that?"

"She left a note. She said you were to help her shop or some such thing. I see you didn't expire from boredom." He reached a hand toward hers, frown turning into a smile so tender she nearly cried out.

But she could not allow his touch now. If he touched her, she'd forget all about her duty, her purpose. If he touched her, she'd throw herself into his arms and pretend she'd never heard of Algernon's plan or Victor Delacorte's threats.

If he touched her, she'd tell him exactly how much she loved him, how much she feared losing him.

She pulled away. "My lord, there is something you must know."

He raised his brows. "You sound so serious. Have you found the *incarnata,* then?"

"The *incarnata?* No, no." She shut her eyes to close off his gentle smile. She couldn't do this. She couldn't see his pleasure turn to pain, his delight to disgust.

"Meredee?"

She opened her eyes to find her regarding her with some concern. "Has something happened to Phoebe?"

Oh, Lord! This is so much harder than I thought.

Meredee put a hand on the table to steady herself. "Your sister isn't here with me, my lord."

He took a step back. "Then where is she?"

There was no hope for her now. "I very much fear that she's run off with my stepbrother, Algernon Whitaker. And I believe Victor Delacorte may be following them."

Chapter Eighteen

A roaring filled Chase's ears, as if the entire contents of Scarborough Bay had poured through him, leaving him empty. "I cannot have understood you correctly," he heard himself say. "Phoebe's run off with Whitaker, not Delacorte?"

She nodded, face tight. "Yes. I believe so. All three of them are missing. But Sir Trevor knows. He's trying to find them."

He should be relieved. He could count on Trev. But he'd thought he could count on the woman before him, too. "And did you say you are related to Whitaker?"

Her gaze met his. "Yes. He's my stepbrother. I owe my living to him."

"I see," he said, but he didn't want to see the picture those words painted. She was completely beholden to Algernon Whitaker, the self-indulgent fop intent on marrying his sister against his wishes. That was where her loyalties must lie.

The one person in the world he'd thought could stand beside him was a sham. Like Phoebe, he had been taken in by a pleasing form and kind, calculated words.

He wanted to shout, to seize the table between them and hurl it across the room, to demand retribution, satisfaction. But she was quite right. She was a woman, and he certainly couldn't challenge her to a duel.

"I'm so sorry," she murmured, her clenching fingers rumpling the embroidery on her yellow overcoat. "I wanted Algernon to tell you. I begged him to tell you. But he was too afraid of what you'd do."

"It seems my fate to be surrounded by people too craven to tell the truth," he said, forcing himself to do nothing more than pick up his gloves. His knuckles stood out as he pulled the leather onto his stiff fingers.

She flinched. "What will you do?"

Was she afraid? Perhaps she should be. The anger inside him was so deep it threatened to swallow him like a black beast. "That, madam," he said, "is no longer your concern." He turned for the door, every muscle tensed, every breath difficult.

She scurried to get in front of him, gray eyes wide and imploring. "Chase, wait. You cannot go after them alone."

The anger forced his tongue. "You dare to protect him? He's taken Phoebe, put her in danger!"

"But I have every reason to believe your sister went willingly. She loves Algernon. She told me so."

Was there no limit to the times this woman could stab him in the heart? "So even Phoebe is given to lying to me."

She raised her chin. "I will not try to justify my actions. But your sister and Algernon hid the truth from you because they believe you will never agree to their suit."

He hurled his hat to the ground, anything to release some of the fire surging through him. "For this very reason! Does running away strike you as the act of two people able to make a successful marriage?"

"No. I fear for the pair of them. But I begin to believe it is not all their fault."

He wouldn't listen to another person tell him how caring for his sister somehow made her behavior acceptable. "Enough. At the moment, I care only about saving Phoebe." He bent and picked up his hat. As he straightened, the room spun, and bile backed up in his throat.

No, not now. I will not be ill.

He must have paled, for she put a hand to his elbow as if to steady him. "My lord, are you all right?"

Of course he wasn't all right. But lashing out at her wasn't going to help matters. He had to think, had to act.

"I'm fine," he snapped. "Where are they?"

"I don't know."

He took a step toward her, and she cringed as if she expected him to strike her. He purposely held himself still. "I'm not going to hurt you, Meredee."

She nodded, straightening. "I know that. But I truly don't know where my stepbrother and your sister are at this moment. Mrs. Price and I searched all of Scarborough. Sir Trevor was doing the same. I fear the reason we cannot find them is that they've headed for Scotland."

"Then I shall do the same." He pushed past her, but she latched onto his arm.

"I'm coming with you."

"No," he said, glaring at her. "You are not."

Unlike Phoebe, unlike that worm Algernon or the dastard Delacorte, she met his look, head high, eyes narrowed to gray lines of determination. "Think, Allyndale!" she said, giving his arm a shake. "If Delacorte or Algernon catches a glimpse of you alone, he'll bolt like a rabbit. And you don't know my stepbrother as I do. I know how he'll travel." She must have felt him hesitate, for her tone softened. "You are barely recovered from your illness. You should not do this alone."

Did he have a choice? It seemed that God intended him to be alone. Yet he knew she was right. Already his anger was fading, to be replaced by a weariness that went to his soul.

"Very well, Miss Price," he said, and she released his arm. "You have two minutes to fetch your pelisse. Meet me in the carriage yard."

She hurried to comply, taking him at his word. Of course, he wasn't the one given to lying.

Meredee flew down the narrow stairs, pulling on her pelisse as she went.

"But you can't just ride off with him," Mrs. Price had protested as Meredee crammed a bonnet onto her head. "Who'll join me for supper?"

"I'm certain you'll find someone," Meredee said, snatching up her gloves. "Surely saving Algernon's life is more important than making polite conversation over roast."

"But you'll be all alone with him in a closed carriage," her stepmother had argued, following her to the door.

"I promise you, madam, the last thing on Lord Allyndale's mind is romance!"

Breath coming in pants, Meredee stopped just long enough to talk to the innkeeper, who was watching two of his guests grumble their way through a game of chess at one of the tables in the common room. "Did Mr. Whitaker call for our carriage?"

Mr. Hollister pursed his plump lips. "Indeed he did, Miss Meredee, not an hour gone. He didn't even wait for your coachman. Said he was in a hurry."

She imagined he was at that, with Chase due at the

inn any moment. She thanked the innkeeper for his trouble and hurried out to the coachyard.

Mrs. Price's fears proved unfounded, for Chase had already dismissed his coachman and was on the box of his elegant green coach.

"Help her up," he ordered his man, and the coachman offered Meredee his cupped hands with a grimace of apology.

She managed to clamber up onto the seat and had barely arranged her skirts when Chase shouted, "Spring 'em!" and the coach jerked forward.

She clutched the sideboard with both hands as they thundered out of the yard and into the street. Chase continued his shouts as they rushed down the lane. Other coaches swerved aside. Sedan chair bearers dashed to the walls. Carts and wagons careened out of their way.

The air whipped past Meredee's face and tugged at her bonnet, but she didn't dare release her hold on the coach for fear she'd go flying, as well.

The turnoff for Scalby was approaching fast. "Which way?" Chase demanded, eyes on his horses.

"To the west," Meredee called back. "He'll make for Thirsk."

He maneuvered the coach easily past the turn and out of the city. The lane led through pastureland with thick hedges on one side and a ditch on the other. As fast as they were going, Meredee couldn't help wondering what would happen should they veer into either.

"He's driving our brown barouche," she shouted against the rushing air. "And Mr. Hollister said Algernon only left a while ago, so we should be able to catch him easily."

He said nothing, merely shook the reins to urge the horses to greater speed. His mouth was a tight line, his jaw clenched. She wasn't sure he even saw the road ahead.

But she saw it. Stepney Hill was approaching, the easy grade rising in the distance. The horses would never take it at this speed.

She reached out and put a hand over his. "My lord, he cannot be far ahead of us, and he doesn't know we're following. There is no need to abuse your horses."

Still he said nothing, but, as she withdrew her touch, he slowed the team. Meredee took a deep breath and managed to pry her other hand from the woodwork.

"Why?" he asked suddenly. "Why does Whitaker persist? Is it the inheritance?"

Meredee sighed, leaning back but finding no comfort against the hard wood of the seat. "No. Algernon is well enough off for most brides. He believes himself to be in love."

"*Love.*" The way he sneered the word made

her want to weep. "Love looks to the other's needs first."

"'Love is patient, love is kind,'" Meredee agreed. "I know. But Algernon believes he is looking to your sister's needs. He thinks he's rescuing her."

He frowned. "From what?"

"From you, my lord."

His hands tightened on the reins, and the well-trained horses sped up again. He reined them back. "I am so very glad to know that the world thinks me such an ogre."

She ignored his sarcasm. "I understand why you kept Lady Phoebe close."

"Apparently not close enough."

And that was her fault, she knew. Would he have agreed to let his sister spend the day with anyone else but the woman who'd saved her life, who'd nursed him back to health?

Who'd given him her heart?

Water pooled at the corners of her eyes, and she knew it wasn't from the wind. But she could not allow tears—not now. Time enough later to mourn what might have been. Now they had to find Algernon and Phoebe, before Delacorte did.

In the next hour, they passed several brown barouches, but all had drivers and none was Algernon. Meredee directed Chase down the path her stepbrother had said he would travel, fearing that with each curve, over each hill, they'd see Algernon just ahead. She had no doubt that the meeting would be explosive. She no longer believed Chase would kill Algernon on sight, but she wasn't sure what he'd do if Lady Phoebe refused to return with him.

They stopped to rest the horses at East Ayton and inquired about Algernon's carriage, but no one had seen it.

"I warn you," Chase said as he helped Meredee back onto the box. "If you've led me in the wrong direction, I will not be responsible for my actions."

Meredee put both hands on the sideboard. "And I warn you, my lord, that I will stand for none of your nonsense when we find them. You will not bully anyone this time."

He slapped the reins and set the team going again.

They were just outside Ruston when Meredee spotted their carriage in the yard of a small inn. "There!" she cried, heart leaping, and Chase pulled the horses into the dusty yard. The inn was low and long, with sparse windows and peeling paint. Besides the barouche, only one other carriage sat in the yard, a yellow curricle with two perfectly matched black horses. Meredee frowned, but Chase leapt off the box.

"My lord!" she cried as he stalked toward the inn, leaving the horses to a groom that had come running.

She could see the effort it cost Chase to stop, to

turn and come back for her. He reached out and lifted her easily from the box. For a moment, she rested in his strength. Once more their gazes locked, held, and this time she saw hurt and doubt written in the blue.

"I'm truly sorry," she murmured.

He looked away and set her down, then turned once more for the inn, and Meredee could only follow.

"Where is the owner of that barouche?" Chase demanded of the tall, stringy innkeeper, who had hurried forward, wiping his hands on his apron.

One look at Chase's face and the fellow pointed wordlessly to a door to their right. Chase strode to it and shoved it open.

Meredee was right behind him. The private parlor was darkly paneled, the fire a dim glow in the hearth. It took a moment for Meredee's eyes to adjust to the gloom. Then she focused on Lady Phoebe, wrapped in her rose-colored pelisse, huddled on a bench by the table, face in her hands. Her sobs were clear over the crackle of the fire. Algernon was down on one knee before her, face set in such harsh lines that Meredee might not have recognized him except for his crimson coat.

"Love?" Chase roared, grabbing Meredee and pulling her into the room as if to force her to see the tableau. "Do you call this love?"

Algernon scrambled to his feet. Phoebe dropped her hands, took one look at her brother and buried her head in her arms on the table beside her.

"Phoebe!" Algernon cried, bending over her.

"Take your hands off her!" Chase ordered, striding into the room.

"Algernon, for God's sake, leave off!" Meredee cried.

Clearly confused, her stepbrother backed away from the girl.

Chase put an arm around his sister and helped her to her feet. She hid her face in his jacket, sobs growing.

What was wrong with the girl? Why didn't she tell Chase that she loved Algernon? Why didn't she defend the man she'd been willing to run away with?

Unless she hadn't been willing. Suspicions drove Meredee to her stepbrother's side. "Algernon, what is this? Tell Lord Allyndale you love Phoebe, that you'd never hurt her."

Chase paused, eyes narrowed at her stepbrother, body tense, daring him to speak.

Algernon raised his head. "I do love your sister, my lord. Despite appearances."

Phoebe shook her head against Chase's waistcoat. "He's lying. He can never love me now, not after what's happened."

"Phoebe!" Algernon cried again, face falling.

Chase's breath came out in a hiss. "Return to Scarborough, Mr. Whitaker. Take your entire family and remove them from my sight. If you come near my sister again, I will press charges." Arm around his sister, he drew her from the room.

Without another word to Meredee.

"Oh, Algernon," she murmured, wrapping her arms about her waist. "What have you done?"

"Nothing," he said, face crumpled and anguished. "I promise you, Meredee! I didn't bring Phoebe here."

"What are you talking about?" Meredee cried. "I warn you, Algernon. You cannot blame someone else for your mistakes."

"Nor is he, Miss Price."

Meredee whirled at the sound of Sir Trevor's voice. He was standing in the doorway, his usually immaculate dove-gray coat speckled with rust-colored dots. As he shoved another man into the room by the collar, she realized the drops were blood.

Sir Trevor's face was hard, his eyes harder, and he gave the man in his grip a little shake. "Mr. Delacorte here must take the blame for abducting Lady Phoebe, or at least attempting to do so. Your stepbrother stopped him."

Algernon cocked a smile. "Sir Trevor had a hand in bringing him to heel. You are very good with your fives, sir."

"Bullies!" Delacorte ranted, head coming up. He was tall and whip-cord thin, all his energy burning from his dark eyes. Meredee thought he might have once been considered handsome, with his russet hair, but now blood trickled from his swelling nose and the skin around his left eye was rapidly turning purple.

"Lady Phoebe is mine," he shouted, "and you stole her from me!"

Sir Trevor tightened his grip on the man's collar, half lifting him off his booted feet so that he choked to a stop. "That is enough. You'll be lucky if you don't hang."

Another man would have blanched or perhaps begged for leniency, but Delacorte merely smiled. The sight sent shivers through Meredee.

"You won't turn me in to the magistrates," he predicted. "This running off has compromised Lady Phoebe. You won't want me to tell the tale. And I expect to be well-paid for my silence." His smile faded, and he squirmed. "Now unhand me!"

Algernon took a step forward, fists bunching, but Meredee put a hand on his arm. Delacorte was clearly deranged. She felt her skin crawl just standing near him. No wonder Chase had worked so hard to protect Phoebe from him.

"I think not," Sir Trevor said quietly. "You will sit in Scarborough's gaol and contemplate your many sins. I will speak to the earl about all this, but don't count on his kindness, for if he doesn't silence you, I will."

Meredee shuddered, but Delacorte did not seem overly troubled. The sly smile stayed on his face as Sir Trevor pulled him from the room.

"Rackety loosescrew," Algernon muttered, then he sighed so heavily Meredee felt it, too. "Come along, Meredee. We may as well return to Scarborough. There's nothing for us here."

Meredee followed him from the room, but, with Chase gone, she very much doubted there was anything for her in Scarborough, either.

Chapter Nineteen

Meredee sat on the box with Algernon as they trundled back to Scarborough. The horses plodded along as if they were as weary as she was. Unlike in her mad dash with Chase, she could have appreciated the scenery, but all she kept seeing was the anger, the piercing blame, in Chase's eyes before he'd swept out with Phoebe.

"I still love her," Algernon said with a dejected sigh. "After all this, I would marry her tomorrow if she'd have me."

"I still don't understand why she won't have you," Meredee answered, hugging her pelisse closer as the day cooled and the breeze from the sea moved inland.

Algernon clucked to the horses. "She's convinced this mess will put me off. Delacorte came on us this afternoon, insisted on a word. He seemed all right, and Phoebe didn't fear him."

She wouldn't, Meredee realized. Chase had sheltered her from the truth.

"Then I saw him force her into her carriage," Algernon continued, "and I knew I had to rescue her. I ran into Sir Trevor at the inn, and he joined me. When we caught up to them, he made them turn aside." He shook his head again. "He can be rather forceful."

"So it seems," Meredee agreed, though the baronet was the least of her concerns.

"The earl may blame me, but I won't give up," Algernon said. He glanced over at Meredee, face brightening. "I know! What if you were to talk to him? He esteems you. Phoebe thinks he may even love you. Tell him what a fine fellow I am, how much I love Phoebe. Surely he'd listen to you."

Meredee stared at him. Had he failed to see the pain etched so clearly on Chase's face? Missed the cutting tone when he'd commanded everyone in Algernon's family to stay away or face the magistrates? Her stepbrother regarded her eagerly, as if nothing had changed.

When everything had changed.

Meredee fixed her gaze out over the horses' heads. "Lord Allyndale never loved me. Nothing I say will move him."

"Why?" She could hear the frown in her stepbrother's words. "What have you done?"

"What have *I* done?" Meredee nearly choked on the words. "I lied to him! I put your needs before the needs of his family. In doing so, I opened the way for Victor Delacorte. Lord Allyndale can only look at me in disgust."

Algernon puffed himself up. "If he sees you as anything less than kind and caring, he's an idiot!"

A laugh forced it way out of her tight throat. "Oh, Algernon, we're the idiots for thinking all this sneaking around would work!"

"And that is my fault. I should never have asked you to get in the middle."

"No, but I'm so glad you did, or I would never have known him." Tears threatened to fall, and she lowered her gaze.

"Now, now," he said, reaching over with one hand to pat hers. "It will all come right, never fear. I'll simply have to talk to the fellow myself."

Meredee closed her eyes. "And you couldn't have done that days ago?"

He withdrew his hand and sighed. "I should have. Forgive me. But I'm bound to do better now. Phoebe fancies herself ruined. I'm her savior, don't you see?"

She'd been Lady Phoebe's savior once, and look what a mess she'd made of everything since then. She hadn't been able to intervene between her stepbrother and Chase; she hadn't been able to keep Lady Phoebe from being kidnapped. Mrs. Price, she was certain, would be only too happy to enumerate the ills she'd suffered without Meredee there to help her. What a miserable savior she'd made.

Did they truly need another Savior?

She hunched her shoulders against the thought. Algernon said this mess was his fault, but she had to accept some share of the blame. She had advised him to flee for Scarborough when he might have tried to reason with Chase. She had agreed to help him hide when she could have insisted that he come out in the open. She'd done everything from a desire to please her family, when the only person she should have been pleasing was God. And He certainly didn't sneak around!

Yet how could she trust God with her future? He never answered her prayers, not the way she wanted them answered. The thought made her stomach heave. Was that the problem? She'd thought there was no point praying for big things because she feared God wouldn't answer. Perhaps she refused to pray because she feared His answers would be contrary to hers.

She bowed her head. *Forgive me, Lord. I know Your thoughts, Your ways, are higher than mine. Show me the plans You have for me. Not my will but Yours be done.*

"Well?" Algernon said, oblivious to her realizations. "What do you think? Won't Allyndale have to agree to my suit with me having saved his sister?"

"A funny thing about being a savior," she said, feeling lighter. "People generally don't thank you for it. And sometimes you may be doing them a disservice."

She thought he would argue, but he nodded. "I know. I had the same argument with Father when he told me he was leaving everything to me. I said he ought to leave you a dowry, at least, but he was afraid of what you'd do with it."

Meredee sucked in a breath. "Did he think me so stupid?"

"Never! But you have a kind heart, Meredee. You help everyone. Father was worried you'd use the fortune to help others and, by doing so, impoverish yourself. And he was afraid if he left it to Mother, she'd spend it all on herself. He knew I would look out for you." He squeezed her hand again. "That's what families do, you know—look out for one another."

The tears fell this time, the breeze cooling them on her cheeks. "Yes, Algernon, I know. Thank you for reminding me."

Chase had barely driven a mile from the inn when he reined in. Phoebe had huddled beside him in such a dejected lump, her sobs throbbing over the drum of the horses' hooves and the jingle of tack, that he could stand it no longer. He tied the reins to the jack and took her in his arms.

She slumped against his chest, her tears dampening his waistcoat, his shirt. What could he say? What should he do? He patted her back, and her sobs only deepened. Every part of him shouted that he must defend, protect, yet there was no one to fight against. He'd never felt so useless.

Meredee would have known how to comfort Phoebe.

He shook his head against the thought, but pictures flashed through his mind like scenes in a play—Meredee, face alight, bending to show him the sea squirts; Meredee, hovering beside him, smile encouraging, while he drank the odious spa water; Meredee on the box beside him, eyes determined, as she warned him she wouldn't stand for his bullying.

Much as he hated to admit it, he knew she could have advised him on how to settle this mess. Meredee would likely have been able to convince him to return to Scarborough instead of driving home like a fox bolting for his den. As it was, he and Phoebe arrived at Allyndale Park after sunset, throwing his remaining staff into a flurry.

"My lord, we didn't expect you," the footman protested. The strapping fellow, who was in charge while Beagan was in Scarborough, had clearly been preparing for bed for his collar was crooked and his coat misbuttoned. "The assistant cook has already retired. Shall I wake her?"

Chase glanced at Phoebe, who shook her head wildly. "I can't eat a thing." She rubbed her arm and sighed. "I wish Meredee was here."

So did he.

And why? He asked himself that question again as he yanked off his cravat in his own room after the footman had helped him off with his boots. She'd proven herself as unreliable as any woman he'd had the misfortune to know. She'd kept her relationship with Whitaker a secret, used her friendship with Chase and Phoebe to aid her stepbrother's cause, put Phoebe in danger from Delacorte, whom he could only hope had been apprehended by Trev. He should be furious with her. Yet he could not forget the sadness, the disappointment in her eyes when he'd left her at the inn.

He'd hurt her, deeply. Was that the mark of a scheming jade? If she wanted to help her stepbrother run off with Phoebe, shouldn't she have looked more triumphant, pressed her advantage? Instead, she'd risked her own reputation to help him find the pair. What kind of deep game was she playing?

Or was she playing at all? Had he completely misjudged the situation? And, more importantly, how was he to set it right?

By the next morning, he had reached no answers, but, as he took a deep breath of the country air, he knew he was glad to be home. Here, things could be ordered to his liking, and his staff were dependable, his steward capable, his tenants reliable, and everyone respectful.

Everyone, that is, except his sister.

"You made a pretty hash of it yesterday," she said when he went to check on her and found her sitting up in bed, lacy cap on her head, sipping hot chocolate.

"Did I?" He came to sit beside her on the canopied bed. He always felt like a lumbering giant in Phoebe's room. The furniture was so dainty, lacquered in white and gilded in gold, and far too many surfaces were lace-covered or pink or both.

"Should I have looked the other way when you disappeared?" he challenged her.

She set her cup on the silver tray in her lap and waved it and the maid away. "Of course not. But you might have asked before lighting into Algernon. He was not the one to blame."

"I refuse to let you protect him," Chase warned.

"You see!" Phoebe pointed a finger at him. "You refuse to listen! You cannot believe that anyone but you might have a single thought in their heads. Well, I will have you know that none of this is Algernon's fault."

He must have looked skeptical, for she pulled her knees up under her lawn nightgown and inched higher until her gaze was even with his. "It's true! If you want someone to blame, it must be Victor Delacorte."

Chase frowned. "Delacorte? What has he to do with this?"

Phoebe spread her hands, face intent. "Everything! He's the one who carried me off to that horrid inn."

Chase recoiled. "What? Explain yourself, miss."

Phoebe dropped back onto her haunches, hands rubbing together in her lap. "Well, you see, I went to visit Meredee, as I told you I would, only Algernon was there. He asked me to go walking with him. I didn't see the harm in that. Oh, Chase, he was so kind and thoughtful, so handsome, so much the gentleman." She sighed dreamily.

Chase pushed his frustration away. "Go on. How does Delacorte figure in all this?"

"He came upon us while we were walking. I was surprised to see him, and I felt a bit guilty, too. You see, I once thought I cared for him, but now I realize it was only a passing fancy."

She could have no idea how young she sounded. "Like many of your suitors," Chase pointed out.

She wrinkled her nose. "Well, perhaps. But I doubt any of them would have behaved like Victor. He looked so shaken to find me with Algernon that I knew I had to speak with him. But when I tried to explain, he went into a temper! He insisted that I accompany him back to the inn to get the curricle so he could take me home."

"And you went with him?" Chase asked with a frown.

She nodded, brows drawn. "I was afraid of what he might do to Algernon if I refused. But when we were in the curricle, he headed out of town. He said I was to marry no one but him, and if he couldn't have me, no one could."

Ice raced along Chase's veins. "Forgive me, Phoebe. I didn't tell you about him because I didn't want you to worry. I thought he might be dangerous, but not like this."

She lowered her gaze with a sigh. "I should apologize to you, too. You tried to protect me, and all I did was fight you. If I hadn't been sneaking around with Algernon, Victor would never have had the chance to approach me."

Chase wasn't so sure about that. "Where's Delacorte now?"

"With Trevor. He and Algernon arrived together."

Chase smiled. "I always said Sir Trevor was a good friend."

"Trevor is very helpful," Phoebe agreed, glancing up with an answering smile. "But it was Algernon who stopped Victor."

Chase's brows went up. "Whitaker?"

"Yes!" The set of Phoebe's chin proclaimed her righteous indignation that Chase would question the prowess of the man she loved. "Algernon was so eloquent in my defense, so confident in the face of danger, that Victor was shamed into backing down." Her face sagged. "But of course he'll never want to marry me now, not with my reputation ruined."

Chase somehow thought the remarkable Mr.

Whitaker would disagree. He rose from the bed. "I'm sure, given time, you'll see that all is not so lost. Until then, perhaps it's wise if we stay here."

Phoebe scrunched up her face. "But what about Scarborough? I'm certain you need to take the waters to return to health."

"I'll be fine. We can return to London in time for Parliament next spring."

"Spring? Are you mad! I cannot stay here that long." She scrambled from the bed. "Please, Chase! I've learned my lesson. No more sneaking about! No more lying."

Chase crossed his arms over his chest. "And exactly what lies have you told, besides hiding Whitaker, of course?"

Phoebe sighed. "I'm not stupid."

Chase frowned, arms dropping. "Whoever said you were?"

"You do!" Phoebe cried, throwing up her hands in a flutter of lace. "And do not deny it," she continued when he opened his mouth to do just that. "You think I'm simple-minded, and I never bothered to disabuse you of the notion. Having you think me dim seemed far easier, on both of us. I didn't have to bother about anything, and you seemed happier when you were protecting me."

Chase snorted. "So you allowed me to worry, to carry your responsibilities all this time, simply because it amused you?"

Her face puckered. "I suppose I did, in a way. But not anymore. I'm beginning to feel as if I've stepped in a noose, and it's tightening. Some days I can scarcely breathe trying to remember to play the fool. Algernon doesn't expect it of me; Meredee chided me for it. It's time you let it go, as well."

Chase stared at her. How had he missed the intelligence in those wide brown eyes, the supreme confidence in that slender body? "You realize I will expect you to show proof of your change of heart," he said.

She nodded. "I know. It's my due, I suppose. I haven't acted honorably. I brought you to Scarborough so I could be near Algernon, and I nearly drowned making his sister's acquaintance. Oh, I've been so silly, and my excuses sound feeble even to me! I suppose I wasn't ready to be the person you wished. But now I want to be a woman of character, a woman Algernon can be proud of, a woman I can be proud of, like Meredee."

Her words haunted him the rest of the morning. Who was this woman looking out of Phoebe's eyes? Had his sister finally taken the step from girl to adult? And who could he praise for helping the transformation? Certainly not him. He'd been too quick to judge her.

And not quick enough to judge himself. Phoebe might have postured to get her own way, but he was no different in wanting things just the way he liked them. He took satisfaction in order, logic, discipline, routine. But there was always more than one way to accomplish a task, and who said his way was the only way? Who even said the task he was trying to accomplish was right?

Only God.

When was the last time he'd asked for advice, sought counsel through prayer or the Bible? Had he even stopped to pray before deciding to marry Meredee? What kind of man had he become that he thought he ruled the world? That anyone who resisted his decrees deserved punishment?

When had he made himself god of his world?

He walked out the front door of the house, raising his footman's brows in the process, and headed out onto the moors. The grasses rippled to the far horizon, open, free. In the stillness, he could hear the mournful cry of the thrush calling for its mate, the rustle of paws as some tiny creature rushed away from him.

Forgive me, Lord. I've set myself up in Your place. I thought it was my duty to protect those around me, to sacrifice myself for them if needed, when You've already paid the greatest price. Show me what You want me to do, with my life, with this illness, with my future. Guide my footsteps in Your paths.

A breeze caressed his cheek, and peace flowed with each step. He knew what he must do. He'd go to Whitaker, talk to the man, learn if he still cared for Phoebe.

And he'd take care of another matter in Scarborough, as well. There was one other person he needed to ask for forgiveness. And he knew just how to do it.

Chapter Twenty

"I still do not understand why you cannot accompany me to the spa," Mrs. Price said, tying the ribbons on her daisy-trimmed straw bonnet. "Algernon may be intent on hiding like a hermit in his cave, but I'm persuaded we could do with some air!"

Meredee glanced to where her stepbrother was bent over the little sitting room table, parchment scattered about him. He'd decided to write a speech that Lord Allyndale could not ignore. He'd started yesterday morning after they'd returned the night before and had been hard at work at it ever since. His dark hair stood on end as if he'd run his hand through it more than once, and he still wore his crimson coat, horridly rumpled now.

"I'd simply prefer a quiet day again today," Meredee murmured, spreading her blue cotton skirts to take a seat at the table, as well. How could she go to the spa, pretend everything was fine, watch the world go on as if nothing had changed? "You will enjoy Colonel Williams's company, I am certain."

"There is that," Mrs. Price allowed. She brightened. "And perhaps without you there he will be emboldened to further our acquaintance. Clever girl!"

Meredee wasn't sure her stepmother was referring to her or to herself, but she smiled as Mrs. Price kissed her cheek and sailed from the room.

"You should have gone with her," Algernon said, crumpling up yet another pierce of parchment. "I'm no kind of company."

"Neither am I," Meredee replied. "But at least we both know the reasons why."

He grunted and dipped his quill in ink once more. Meredee watched him a moment, listening to the scratch of the nib against the sheet. She'd prayed much of yesterday and twice more since rising, yet still answers eluded her. She felt as if someone had a fist in her back, urging her up, out. Yet where was she supposed to go? What was she supposed to do?

She rose and paced the room, three steps to the window and three steps to the table. Back and forth, back and forth, her brain moving as quickly as her steps. The rustle of her gown eclipsed the sound of the quill.

"I wish you'd stop doing that," Algernon muttered. "It's hard to concentrate."

Meredee smiled. "Now you know how everyone else feels when you pace."

Algernon glanced up with a smile. But before he could answer her, a knock sounded at the door. They both stared at the yellow-painted panel.

Algernon set down his quill. "I suppose I should get that."

"No, no," Meredee said, hurrying to the door. "It's probably just Mr. Hollister, the innkeeper, asking if we want anything. I'll get it." She opened the door.

Chase stood on the other side. His black coat outlined his powerful body; his craggy face was stern. Still, at the sight of him she felt a jolt that threatened to rock her off her feet.

He removed his top hat. "May I come in?"

She couldn't find her voice. Behind her, she heard Algernon's chair scrape the floor as he rose. "Let him in, Meredee. I'm ready for him."

Chase's face tightened. She wanted to shove him out the door and pull him closer at the same time. But she knew this had to be Algernon's fight. She stepped aside and let Chase in.

He nodded to her stepbrother, stripping off his driving gloves and laying them and his hat on the table. "Whitaker."

"Allyndale." Algernon raised his chin. "I intended to come see you today. I owe you an explanation."

Chase raised a brow. "Yes, you do."

Algernon nodded as if satisfied they'd agreed on at least this much. He stood stiffly, his coat a wash of blood against the yellow of the room. Chase stood just as stiffly, his shoulders broader, his stance wider, as if aching for a fight. Could they agree on anything so important as Lady Phoebe's future? Or hers? The stretching silence pulled at her senses.

"Gentlemen," Meredee said, eyeing them each in turn, "I suggest you get on with it."

She thought Chase's mouth quirked. Was he fighting a smile? She hated the hope that sprang up in her heart.

"Very well," Algernon said, feet shuffling just the slightest as if he longed to pace. "First, I want you to know that I would never do anything to harm your sister, Allyndale. That's why when you first rejected my suit, I left London."

"Very gentlemanly of you," Chase said, "running away."

Algernon paled. "You are not a man to cross, my lord."

"Yet cross me you did."

And so had she. She'd feared just such a fierce look from him, thought she might flee from it. Now she wasn't sure what to think, what to feel. She could see heartache looming in every direction.

Take a step. Follow me.

Algernon took a step closer to him. "I only resisted you when it became apparent how unhappy your sister was. I could not stand by and watch her be made a prisoner in her own home."

Was Meredee a prisoner, too, of fear? She could

see a muscle working in Chase's jaw. She thought he might argue with Algernon, but instead he merely said, "So you effected a prison break."

Algernon shook his head. "No, my lord. Your sister came to me. She let me know that she returned my love and wanted nothing more than to be my wife." He lowered his gaze and fingered the sheet of parchment on the table. "To my sorrow, I did not take her up on her generous offer. I insisted that we must wait, that we must win your approval."

"That you must use your sister's influence to sway me."

Chase said the words so calmly, so coolly, that Meredee could almost believe he didn't care. Yet each word cut through her emotions like a knife. "I never pled his cause," she felt compelled to put in. "I never sang his praises."

Chase glanced at her. His face remained composed, but some emotion crouched in his eyes. Before she could name it, he looked away. "No, you simply pointed out that I was keeping my sister too close, even after you knew the reason why."

If that's what he believed, then he'd never known her. She squared her shoulders against the pain.

"Delacorte," Algernon said. "The rotter. Sir Trevor explained the situation to me on the road. But you mustn't blame Meredee, my lord. She had no idea he was in town or that he was dangerous."

"Actually, she knew both," Chase said before she

could explain to Algernon. "I spoke with Sir Trevor yesterday. He told me she searched tirelessly for you and Phoebe. And her warning to him allowed him to be in the right place to intercept you."

Once more he was making her sound the savior, but she would not allow herself to fall into that trap again. "I started searching for Algernon," she told him, "because I wanted him to tell you the truth before you came to call on me."

Chase gazed toward the window, as if the sun or the sky could somehow answer him. "And why was that?"

Oh, but she would not answer. She could not tell him how she'd hoped for his love, not after what had passed between them, not when he was clearly here to judge.

Algernon answered for her. "Because she'd been trying to convince me to tell you for days, and I wouldn't listen."

"Then why tell me all now, Mr. Whitaker? Why not show me the door?"

"Because I love Phoebe!" Meredee winced at his shout, but Algernon ran both hands through his hair, forcing it to stand on end. "Have you heard nothing I've ever said to you? I adore your sister! She's clever and warm, and her beauty outshines the sun. She is a paragon among women, and I wish you'd just consent to let me offer for her hand in marriage!"

Meredee brought both hands to her mouth to

smother the nervous laugh that threatened to escape. After laboring all night, that was the best her stepbrother could manage? Chase would eat him for supper.

Across the room, Chase raised his chin and looked at Algernon down his nose, his gaze sharp and assessing. No! She would not allow this to end in a duel after all, even if she had to jump between them and force them apart.

"Very well, Mr. Whitaker," Chase said. "Ask her."

Algernon blinked, arm half raised as if to threaten dire consequences at a refusal. He slowly lowered his arm. "You mean it?"

He did. Meredee could see it in the light that brightened his eyes. Her hands fell away from her mouth as relief washed over her. *Thank You, Lord!*

"I am a man of my word, Whitaker," Chase said. "Phoebe's at the estate now, waiting for you. I told her my intentions in coming here today. She was hoping for just such an outcome."

Algernon glanced at Meredee, face alight. His joy spilled over her as he reached out and seized Chase's hand. "I don't know how to thank you, my lord," he stammered, pumping Chase's hand over and over. "I promise to take the best care of her."

"I would expect no less," Chase said, managing to disengage. "But be advised. I told Phoebe I would stand for no less than a year's engagement."

Algernon's face fell. "A year?"

"A year, sir. I have known my sister since the day she was born, and yesterday I learned I never knew her at all. I want to make sure that you both have time to appreciate each other's character before marrying. If your feelings are unchanged a year from now, you will have my blessing." He bent closer. "But not a day sooner, sir, or we may yet meet across that dueling field."

Algernon nodded. "Agreed. And let me say that you have made me the happiest of men." He looked again at Meredee. "Do you hear that, Meredee? I'm to be married!"

Meredee had to smile. Algernon, it seemed, had been granted his fondest wish. She still wasn't sure what to do about hers. "I heard," she said. "Congratulations. But perhaps you'd better ask Phoebe before you make the announcement."

He struck his forehead with the heel of one hand. "Phoebe! Of course I must ask Phoebe. I'll borrow a horse immediately." He started for the door, then stopped suddenly and looked back at Meredee, uncertain. "That is, if you don't need me."

His kindness warmed her, but before she could answer, Chase spoke up. "Your sister is in good hands, Mr. Whitaker. I suggest you leave before I change my mind."

She shook her head. There went her irresistible earl, taking command of the situation. Algernon must have felt the same way, for he straightened. "You cannot intimidate me, my lord," he said, though his voice cracked on the last word. "Meredee, do you wish to speak with this gentleman?"

Did she? Chase's face was blank; his eyes told her nothing. He held his emotions deeply, where no one could reach them. Yet suddenly she knew she wanted to reach them. She wanted to be near him, to share confidences, to feel the brush of his hand against hers. She couldn't let him walk away. If God had given her this opportunity, she would not waste it.

I'm taking a step, Lord.

"Yes, Algernon," she said. "I believe you can leave me safely in Lord Allyndale's company."

He walked back to face Chase. "You will be kind to my sister, my lord. Or we may yet meet across the dueling field."

"Understood, Mr. Whitaker," Chase said, inclining his head with something akin to respect. "I will be a gentleman, I promise you."

Algernon nodded as if satisfied and left the room.

And the space immediately felt smaller, the yellow walls close, the wood furniture tiny. Only a few feet separated her from Chase. He stood watching her, waiting. Could she cross that space? What should she say? Would he be as forgiving of her misdeeds as he was of Algernon's?

"I believe I owe you an apology," he said.

He owed *her* an apology? Her emotions came crashing down around her, and her knees started shaking. She clutched at the wall behind her to remain upright.

He strode to her side. "Meredee? Are you all right?"

She nodded, but he scooped her up in his arms as if she weighed nothing and carried her to the closest chair. She closed her eyes, breathed in his scent, let the heat from his body warm her. *I've never wanted anything so much, Lord. But not my will but Yours be done.*

"Is it your head?" he murmured, setting her down on the chair. She opened her eyes to find him hovering over her, face tight with concern. "Or your stomach? Do you feel faint? I will never forgive myself if I've passed this cursed illness on to you!"

"No, no," Meredee managed. She realized she was still gripping his jacket and released it, the warm wool falling away from her fingers. "I'm not ill. I'm just astonished. I was afraid you'd be furious with me."

He sighed and stepped back. "Forgive me, both for making you think I was so hardhearted and for being so hardheaded. Phoebe says I've made a mess of things, and I begin to think she's right."

She bit back a smile. "Phoebe always thinks she's right, my lord."

He chuckled, and she wanted to clutch the sound to her heart, never release it. "I'm beginning to understand that, too. I wish your stepbrother the very best of luck."

"So do I. But I believe love can make a difference."

"Yes," he murmured, "it can."

Her heart started beating faster. "Then may I take it that I, too, am forgiven? I withheld the truth from you. I'm sorry."

"You were put in an untenable position. I see that now. When I first learned the truth, I lashed out without thinking."

"Because you had been betrayed before. I understand."

"You are always understanding. That is one of your great gifts, Meredee. And to prove to you that I understand, I wanted to give you something."

She started to refuse, but he reached into his coat, drew out a long wooden box and held it out to her.

"Take it," he said with a smile when she hesitated. "I promise it won't bite."

She took it slowly, turning it to see all sides. It was carved with vines and roses, the work delicate and intricate. "It's lovely."

"I hope you'll like what's inside better."

Inside. She swallowed. With great care, she lifted the lid. There, cradled in brown velvet, lay the *incarnata*. The shell was tinged a warm salmon pink, the sides curved gently up to the tip. She swore she could feel the heat of the sun, hear the hush of the waves just looking at it.

We did it, Papa. We found it!

Meredee drew a shaky breath. "Where did you get it?"

"I found it. I remembered what you'd said about not purchasing it, but I thought perhaps you would accept a gift from a friend. You'd mentioned the northern shores might be more likely spots. I spent the better part of yesterday searching, but God rewarded me with the morning tide."

Reward indeed. He'd searched for it, just for her. Did he know how much that meant to her?

"It isn't perfect," he murmured, bending closer. "You can see it's rough along the edges. But then, so am I."

Meredee ran a finger along the curve of the shell. "It seems perfect to me."

"Make no mistake, Meredee. No one can live up to expectations of perfection." He strode away from her, pacing the room with quick steps. She was reminded of her stepbrother. But Chase's black coat was far less dashing than Algernon's, his cravat tied far more simply. And as for his boots…

Why, they were coated in mud.

Meredee rose. "Chase! You muddied your boots!"

He shrugged, but his smile spoke volumes. "It seemed a small price to pay to please you. I do love you, you know."

Meredee stood there, heart too full to allow her to speak. *Oh, Lord, thank You! This was the biggest prayer of all, and You honored it.* Tears started, but this time they were only the overflow of the joy that bubbled up inside her. Was this the true reason her father loved his shells, why he'd left them to her, of all people? They weren't just scientific specimens, but the cups of memory, reminding him of places he'd been, people he'd loved. This shell wasn't for her father; it was for her and Chase. She laid it tenderly back into the box with trembling fingers.

Chase strode back to her side and took her hands, cradling them close. "Please don't cry. I never meant to hurt you. I told you I'm not much for poetry, but perhaps I can find a better way to show you how much you've come to mean to me."

"Nonsense," she said, smiling through her tears. "I think you said that brilliantly. I only wish I had some way of showing you how very much I love you in return."

"Oh, Meredee." He gathered her close, resting his head against her hair. "You say it every day, in every smile, every encouraging word, every act of kindness. I'm sorry it took me so long to see that. I may be a bit of a bully, but with you beside me, I know I'm a better man. Marry me, Meredee. I'll do all I can to make you happy."

She closed her eyes, leaned into his strength. "Oh, Chase, yes!"

His lips brushed hers in a solemn promise. Nestled against him, she knew she was right where God wanted her, right where she'd dreamed of being, right where she was meant to stay.

Chapter Twenty-One

"Everyone must want to see you." Phoebe's whisper bounced off the golden stone arches inside St. Mary's Church as the girl stood beside Meredee at the back of the chapel. "There must be at least a hundred people here."

Meredee knew. She could hear the rustle of lustring, the whisper of muslin and the occasional murmur; catch glimpses of tall hats and ribboned bonnets around the stone pillars that held the arches. So many of Scarborough's inhabitants had taken Chase up on his offer to come to their wedding that she was once again a seven-day wonder.

"Let them look," she murmured to Phoebe. "Today I am so happy nothing can trouble me."

On Meredee's other side, Algernon, in a coat of a muted blue she was sure would offend his sensibilities any other day, grinned. "I think when we marry," he teased Phoebe, "we'll have to try for Westminster. Half of London will want to attend!"

Meredee wasn't so sure of that, but a lot could happen in a year. Look at what had happened since Chase had proposed a month ago. They'd planned a wedding and a future and were ready to start both with God's blessing.

Oh, they'd had a few bumps. Mrs. Price had vacillated between tears and squeals of joy when Meredee had told her about Chase's proposal.

"A countess!" she'd enthused, daubing at her eyes with a handkerchief. "You will live in a fine house. I'm sure he'll want to gown you properly. You must ask Algernon if he knows any good seamstresses." She'd paused to gaze at Meredee, lips trembling. "Oh, but how shall I get on without you?"

It was Chase who found the solution. "She is welcome to live with us, but I think she would vastly prefer being independent," he'd said when Meredee had broached the subject the next day. "We'll find her a suitable companion and install her in my London house. If we need to go to town, we can always rent rooms."

Both Meredee and Mrs. Price were pleased with the arrangement. "Though, mind you, I don't imagine any companion can take your place," Mrs. Price said to Meredee when she broached the matter with her stepmother. She patted Meredee's cheek and sighed.

"There's no one who can soothe my headaches as you do."

But Meredee was more concerned about Chase's headaches. As the days went by, he only grew stronger, and she saw no signs of the illness returning. Just to be sure, they'd journeyed with Phoebe to Edinburgh for a few days' consultation with a prominent physician there. The man had given Chase a clean bill of health.

"Keep your windows closed at night and mind yourself when travelling on the moors," he'd advised. "There is growing evidence that this fever is caused by the bite of an insect. Keep your skin covered."

"Or wear my father's insect repellent," Meredee had teased Chase after they left, then laughed at the face Chase made.

The one dark spot on her happiness was the future of Victor Delacorte. Chase and Sir Trevor agreed that the man was a danger, to others and perhaps to himself, but, contrary to Sir Trevor's recommendation, Chase had decided not to press charges. Sir Trevor had remanded Delacorte into the custody of the man's parents, who promised to have him watched at one of their estates in the country. Meredee could only hope the quieter life would help return the fellow to his senses in time.

Now Phoebe stiffened and arranged her rose satin skirts. The vicar had taken his place on the altar, his long face warmed by his smile. The sounds of the crowd hushed, stilled, until Meredee was certain the loudest noise in the lofty chapel was the sound of her heart beating.

She was getting married.

The vicar glanced first to the right and then down the center aisle, his smile widening as his gaze lit on Meredee. She smoothed down the ivory satin of her gown, tugged at the lace edging her long sleeves. It was time to take her place as well, at Chase's side.

"Here we go!" Phoebe whispered, then started out. Meredee accepted Algernon's arm to follow, moving from shadow to golden light. Murmurs rose again, and she knew people were craning their necks for a glimpse of her. Her gown whispered along the stone floor behind her.

As they approached the altar, the space opened, and she caught sight of Chase, waiting for her. He towered over the vicar, broad shoulders encased in blue, legs wrapped in dove-gray breeches. She swore she could feel his confidence even from here.

She ought to be nervous, with so many eyes on her, with his gaze so open, so admiring. She ought to tremble, to hesitate. Yet every step felt right, every moment an end to the life she had known, every breath an opportunity to thank God for making her dreams—even those she'd been afraid to offer Him—come true.

She met Chase before the altar, the stone arches sweeping away on either side. With an irresistible smile that was all for her, he took her hand, and they turned to the vicar to become what they already were in their hearts.

Husband and wife.

* * * * *

Dear Reader,

Thank you for choosing *The Irresistible Earl*. I hope you enjoyed the story of two people so determined to help others that they very nearly missed their chance at love.

God's certainly helped the town of Scarborough over the years. The spa waters were first discovered in the 1600s by a local widow. Damage from storms and sea surges in 1808 and 1836 required the main spa building to be completely rebuilt. The spa was expanded and made more grand in 1839 and 1858, only to be destroyed by fire in 1876. Town officials rebuilt again in 1879 and opened the current historic buildings in 1880. The town still welcomes visitors intent on playing on the beach and indulging in the waters of the spa.

I welcome visitors to my website too. Please feel free to contact me via www.reginascott.com, where you can also read about my upcoming books.

Blessings!
Regina Scott

QUESTIONS FOR DISCUSSION

1. Meredee's stepbrother, Algernon, asks her to spy on the Earl of Allyndale for him. Has anyone in your family ever put you in a difficult position? How did you handle it?

2. Meredee feels her life is trapped in a pattern she is powerless to break. Have you or someone you know felt this way? What did you do about it?

3. God calls us to serve one another. Is there ever a point where you can serve too much?

4. What do you think Chase and Meredee learned about helping others by the end of the book?

5. Lady Phoebe hides her true character behind a giggle. Is it ever right to conceal our true nature?

6. Chase feels called to protect his sister. When does such care become overprotection?

7. Mrs. Price equates financial security with emotional security. What is the proper place of financial concerns in our lives?

8. Meredee first sees her father's shells as the handiwork of God. Where do you most often see the Father's hand?

9. Later, Meredee comes to realize that the shells hold memories of places she's been and people she loves. What other objects do we use to collect memories?

10. Meredee and Chase both have doubts about Phoebe and Algernon's ability to forge a happy marriage. What does it take to create a solid marriage? Do you think Chase and Meredee will have that kind of marriage? What about Phoebe and Algernon?

INSPIRATIONAL

Inspirational romances to warm your heart & soul.

Love Inspired.
HISTORICAL

TITLES AVAILABLE NEXT MONTH

Available July 12, 2011

CALICO BRIDE
Buttons and Bobbins
Jillian Hart

FRONTIER FATHER
Dorothy Clark

SECOND CHANCE FAMILY
Winnie Griggs

HEARTS IN FLIGHT
Patty Smith Hall

REQUEST YOUR FREE BOOKS!

2 FREE INSPIRATIONAL NOVELS
PLUS 2
FREE
MYSTERY GIFTS

Love Inspired

HISTORICAL
INSPIRATIONAL HISTORICAL ROMANCE

YES! Please send me 2 FREE Love Inspired® Historical novels and my 2 FREE mystery gifts (gifts are worth about $10). After receiving them, if I don't wish to receive any more books, I can return the shipping statement marked "cancel". If I don't cancel, I will receive 4 brand-new novels every month and be billed just $4.24 per book in the U.S. or $4.74 per book in Canada. That's a saving of at least 23% off the cover price. It's quite a bargain! Shipping and handling is just 50¢ per book in the U.S. and 75¢ per book in Canada.* I understand that accepting the 2 free books and gifts places me under no obligation to buy anything. I can always return a shipment and cancel at any time. Even if I never buy another book, the two free books and gifts are mine to keep forever.

102/302 IDN FDCH

Name	(PLEASE PRINT)	

Address		Apt. #

City	State/Prov.	Zip/Postal Code

Signature (if under 18, a parent or guardian must sign)

Mail to the Reader Service:
IN U.S.A.: P.O. Box 1867, Buffalo, NY 14240-1867
IN CANADA: P.O. Box 609, Fort Erie, Ontario L2A 5X3

Not valid for current subscribers to Love Inspired Historical books.

Want to try two free books from another series?
Call 1-800-873-8635 or visit www.ReaderService.com.

* Terms and prices subject to change without notice. Prices do not include applicable taxes. Sales tax applicable in N.Y. Canadian residents will be charged applicable taxes. Offer not valid in Quebec. This offer is limited to one order per household. All orders subject to credit approval. Credit or debit balances in a customer's account(s) may be offset by any other outstanding balance owed by or to the customer. Please allow 4 to 6 weeks for delivery. Offer available while quantities last.

Your Privacy—The Reader Service is committed to protecting your privacy. Our Privacy Policy is available online at www.ReaderService.com or upon request from the Reader Service.

We make a portion of our mailing list available to reputable third parties that offer products we believe may interest you. If you prefer that we not exchange your name with third parties, or if you wish to clarify or modify your communication preferences, please visit us at www.ReaderService.com/consumerschoice or write to us at Reader Service Preference Service, P.O. Box 9062, Buffalo, NY 14269. Include your complete name and address.

LIHI1